GLORIFIED

THE SAGA OF THE NANO TEMPLAR BOOK THREE

JON DEL ARROZ

RISLANDIA BOOKS

ONE

Drin parried the attack with little effort. His opponent chopped down at him with her light sword in a haphazard motion, easy to defend against. If Drin wished it, he could have delivered a kick to his opponent's torso, thrown her off guard, and stabbed her through the eye without breaking a sweat.

To an outsider, the sparks flying off the two energy weapons meeting would have appeared to be an impressive sight. The orange light reflected on the woman's furred face, her eyes tense with concentration, her lips pressed together. They had both formed their nanites into loose-fitting practice attire, having no need to don full battle armor.

In an ordinary battle, he would have sliced her into bits before she readied herself for her next blow. She wasn't ready for someone of his caliber. For now, he stayed on defense, allowing the woman to get a feel for the blade. She lacked the advantage of having been trained since being a young child with weapon in hand. Some people had to learn late. Drin could only hope it wasn't too late for her.

"Good," Drin said, despite thinking her form was anything but.

She'd made improvements over the last time, which was the important part. "Watch your footwork. Keep yourself balanced so you can move fluidly."

"It's like dancing," said Anais, the woman across from him. She had long, floppy ears, which drooped over the sides of her head. She sweated through her white fur, causing her gray attire to cling to her lithe body.

It was distracting, but Drin tried to keep his focus away from her form. He had his vows of celibacy to consider, and Anais already tempted him far too much without his own stray thoughts aiding the effort. He pushed forward with his light sword, causing her to stumble backward. "Remember, when the two blades meet, you can use your body weight as if you were pushing on another object. Many swordsmen forget this with light swords, which you can use to your advantage."

Anais frowned, narrowing her eyes on him. "I don't think I'll ever be as good as you."

"Perhaps not, but Lord willing, you'll be able to hold your own."

She unleashed a flurry of blows on him, moving at a much more rapid pace than he could manage. Deklyn were faster than the Elorians as a whole. If she were a normal member of her species, Drin might have been able to match or even exceed her speeds with the help of the nanites, but she also had the advantage of the same ancient nanotechnology, which made the Templars the most notorious fighting force in the galaxy. Her speed made up for her inexperience and lesser strength.

Even with her rapid assault, Drin parried her every attack. He could see Anais was getting frustrated from an inability to pierce his defenses. She hadn't struck a single blow which penetrated the shielding his nanites provided. The way her face tightened into impatience amused him. It reminded him of when he had to spar with his instructors as a teenager. He laughed.

"It's not..." Anais delivered her hardest strike to him yet, "...funny!"

"I'm sorry," Drin said. "Your face. If you could only see it..." He blocked the attack and pushed, forcing her off balance again. He thrust forward, a strike that if he had intended on hitting her would have killed her, but he intentionally let his blade slip to her side and past her. "Don't get angry during a fight. If you do, you'll allow your opponent an advantage. You need to keep your focus and calm."

"It's not as easy as it sounds," Anais spat back at him. She took in several deep breaths, circling him as she regained her composure.

She moved with the speed of the wind. Drin hadn't been ready for her to recover so quickly. Her movements were so rapid he couldn't draw his sword back in time to block this time. She struck to his side, causing his nanite field to react and capture the energy. It created a flickering pink glow around him.

Though the nanite field absorbed the shock, it couldn't completely dissipate the weapon's attack. It felt as if a wooden practice sword whacked him hard in the side, causing him to wince and stumble away from Anais's light sword.

"My God, are you okay?" Anais asked. She let her weapon dissipate, and she rushed to him, touching his off-hand arm gently. In the middle of a battle, it would have been a foolish move, though Anais didn't show the penchant for sustained combat. She empathized too much with other beings' pain. A noble trait, but one which would get her killed if she faced Sekarans with such a naive outlook.

Drin had to teach her a lesson.

He dragged his foot across the gravel, sweeping Anais' legs out from under her. She gasped as she lost her footing, falling to the ground and crashing onto her rear. The fall jolted her, and had to have hurt, given her expression, but her eyes filled with a blood rage, fire she'd displayed before.

She swept her own leg across the ground, causing Drin to lose his footing along with her. Not expecting her retaliation, Drin wobbled his arms to try to keep his balance, but to no avail. His light sword dissipated, an auto-defensive measure so Templars didn't inadvertently stab themselves when they lost control.

Drin fell forward.

He dropped over Anais, barely able to brace himself and keep his weight from crushing her, with his palms hitting the gravel. His hands would sting for days as a reminder of his failure, but that wasn't what made the moment one he would remember.

Anais's black, Deklyn eyes stared at him, wide, beautiful, like black holes that could suck a man into them, and he'd never be able to return. And she was so close to him. Her whole body under his. As her chest rose and fell with her heavy breathing, her body brushed against his, giving him a tingling sensation he hadn't experienced before.

Her breathing was warm on his neck. It tickled, but in a pleasant way. It made Drin feel *good*. Too good. He immediately rolled to the side to extricate himself from the position, falling the rest of the way to the ground and lying on his back. He kept his eyes skyward and breathed in and out several times to try to purge himself of the sensation.

"Templar Drin? Is everything okay?" a voice asked. Drin looked up to see another person, a six-armed Skree, muscular, with a purple hue to his skin. It was Err-dio, the Skree who came with him and the Templars to this planet, pressing himself into service as Drin's squire.

It was odd for Drin to have what amounted to an apprentice and a servant, but Err-dio served faithfully. He was always there when Drin needed him, including this moment. As the Skree came closer, he offered one of his six arms to assist Drin to his feet.

"I'm fine. Simply instructing Anais in the ways of combat," Drin said, dusting himself off after he stood.

Err-dio had already moved to help Anais.

"You're supposed to offer your hand to the lady first," Anais said.

Err-dio frowned. "Is that a law in the Holy Book? I admit I have not studied the entirety of its contents as of yet. I have tried, but the genealogies of the Elorian Tribes at the beginning of the Holy Gospel of L'thue are very difficult to get through. I find myself falling asleep after reading all of the names."

Anais giggled, much more amused than Drin found the situation to merit.

"No, it's not in the Holy Book," she said, "but it is part of basic courtesy. Don't you treat women with respect on your home planet?"

Even though Anais was clearly teasing, Err-dio didn't seem to register it. He gasped, placing a hand over his chest. "I am very respectful toward women. However, among the Skree, you assist the person with a higher station first, it doesn't matter what sex the person is."

This conversation couldn't go well. Drin cleared his throat. "You must have come out this way for a reason, yes? I can't imagine you wanted to watch Anais and me train with light swords."

Err-dio beamed. "I gather there's much I could learn from listening to you instruct others. Perhaps there's some I could learn from Anais as well. Her leg move was rather unorthodox but very effective."

Drin rubbed the side of his leg he had landed upon. "You're right about that," he said.

"But yes, I did come here for more than a social call," Err-dio said. "Father Cline sent me to retrieve you and bring you back to the *Justicar*. The Church has an assignment for us."

Though Anais tried to hide her expression, Drin could read

her like a book. The blood drained from her face. "Is this about the superweapon Father Cline mentioned the Sekarans had obtained?"

Weeks ago, Father Cline briefed both Drin and Anais on an intelligence operation that had discovered a new Sekaran weapon, one dangerous enough to destroy whole worlds. He said they needed more time to formulate a plan of attack before they deployed to fight the Sekarans, but it was possible the time had come.

Err-dio shrugged. "I don't know, I was just sent to retrieve you."

Drin glanced between the two. In some ways, they were both his apprentices, but if the Templars had to leave soon, it would be possible Anais wouldn't come with him. He'd spent so much time with her in recent months that he didn't relish the thought, but all things changed with time. It wasn't his place to yearn for her company, even if a small tug on his heart wanted him to dwell on the thought. "We'll have to end our training here for now," Drin said. "Thank you for being a diligent student."

Anais' eyes twinkled at him. "Thank you," she said softly.

Drin nodded. He wouldn't say goodbye. He couldn't believe this would be the last he'd see of her.

Err-dio turned to lead the way through the city streets to the Deklyn spaceport. They would find out what Father Cline needed soon enough.

TWO

ANAIS CONTINUED TO WORK WITH HER LIGHT SWORD FOR several minutes after Drin and Err-dio departed. She assumed the proper stance, moved like she had been taught, but it wasn't the same without Drin there to counter her blows. Her light sword danced through the air, humming as it slid gracefully in front of her. It was either keep working or stare after Drin as he departed. She couldn't let her eyes linger on him, not after they'd been so close together.

When he'd fallen atop her, Anais could sense his longing for her. If they'd had less willpower, they would have kissed. If only he would have, she would be able to shed months of repressed frustration. It nearly drove her mad.

But he had an oath of celibacy. She understood this fact and never pressed him for the physical contact she desired from him. Only, learning he desired her as well... It complicated matters. It shouldn't, but the knowledge made her yearn for him all the more.

He didn't seem to be aware of her ability to read his emotions. The additional sense came to her after Drin had healed her and saved her life in the middle of a battle. Her nanites communicated with those in close proximity to her, including those of others. Did all Elorians have this ability and not realize it?

There was so much to learn about the little machines pulsing through her body. She could spend a lifetime studying them, but they would have to wait. She had other important and immediate matters to deal with, and it wasn't as if her nanites would be leaving her any time soon.

Anais let her light sword dissipate in the air, turning from her makeshift practice area on her mansion's grounds to head to the city library—the place she'd established Deklyn's new government of Merchant Lords. It was a new building, the old library having collapsed from when Drin cut its support pillars to bring them down atop invading Sekarans.

Entering the large structure situated between two trees, Anais could smell the scent of recently installed carpet and fresh paint. It was nice to have a new building, though Anais missed the old in some ways. All of the surviving equipment and remaining repository of information had been moved into the space during the last three days. Dozens of people scurried about, working.

Lyssa, her friend since childhood, occupied an office behind a glass wall. She conversed on a holo in front of her, negotiating new trade contracts. Most of the surrounding inhabited systems had cut ties with Deklyn during the Sekaran occupation, which made her have to work from scratch to bring traders back to the world.

The Sekarans had caused such destruction, killed so many people. It was overwhelming to think about.

Anais waited at the door until Lyssa finished her call, and then she slipped inside. "Working again?" Anais said.

"Always," Lyssa said. She had light brown fur, unlike Anais's pale white. "And you're just getting here." She glanced at her chrono. "It's afternoon."

"Doesn't mean I haven't been working. Drin wanted to train me with the nanites." Anais crossed her arms over her chest.

"He wants to train you, alright," Lyssa said.

"What does that even mean?"

A moment of silence filled the air before Lyssa burst out laughing. "Never mind. Your face is turning bright red and it says it all. I won't tease you anymore. But we could use more of your time and attention. We're finally getting a lot of the world organized and it's a daunting task for the six of us."

By the six of them, she meant the other children of the former Merchant Lords, including herself, Krytien, Elaym, Manil, Dawn, and Morgon. Their parents had all run this world and all of the trade coming to and from it for decades before the Sekarans slaughtered all of them mercilessly.

It was amazing so many of their children survived. There had been over a dozen families among the merchant lords before, people Anais had seen in passing when she was busy with her studies—and her social life. She wished she'd spent more time seeing what their predecessors *did* and learning who they were. It would have been so helpful to have the experience.

"I know. I might be helping sooner rather than later."

"Why's that?"

"I don't know. Drin was summoned to his ship. I think he's not going to be here much longer."

"That's too bad," Lyssa said. "But if it helps you focus..."

"Hey," Anais said, narrowing her eyes.

Lyssa grinned. "Sorry. It's too easy." The smile dropped from her face. "I could use a little help trying to find contacts, though. We need to restore trade to the planet, and I've been doing my best, but most worlds have heard of the Sekaran attack here and want to stay away from us, to not draw their attention. I've run out of people to reach out to."

"I can't say I blame them," Anais said. If she were in their positions, she wasn't sure she'd want to draw their attention either. But if Lyssa was asking for help, when she was so good at negotiations, it meant she really needed it. "Let me think about it. I don't really remember anyone my father talked to from before... I wish I'd paid more attention."

"I think we all wish we could change the way we were," Lyssa said, scrunching her nose.

"It was fun at the time, though." Anais tapped her fingers on Lyssa's desk. "There's Nagell, the CEO of Parthenon Station. Have you talked with him?"

"I've tried to call, but the station's comm officer keeps forcing me to leave messages."

Anais frowned, considering. Should they send someone to meet with him directly? When they needed help the last time, Parthenon Station's resources had worked for them. Nagell had set them up with the funds to hire the mercenaries who helped liberate Deklyn from Sekaran rule. "We could send a delegation to the station."

"But who? All of us are strapped for time trying to figure out how to restore order and run this whole world." Lyssa motioned in a wide sweep. "I've got so many calls I don't even have time to talk to you right now. And Elaym is traveling across all the continents trying to make sure the people stay calm. We don't even have a way to track crime right now."

The frustration came through in her voice, and Anais didn't want to add to it. She wanted to help, and it made her feel guilty that she hadn't done her part to assist everyone these past weeks. She'd tried, but she had been coming in in the afternoon, with Drin training her in the morning. One couldn't lead a planet as a part time job. But they'd managed without her so far. Lyssa had said as much. They wanted more of her help, but what if she could help in ways they didn't consider? "I could go."

Lyssa opened her mouth as if she were going to argue, but then closed it again. She cocked her head at Anais, a curious expression on her face. "You know, it's not a half-bad idea. We could recruit someone else for the domestic work. You might be able to persuade Nagell to help us. He seems to like you."

"You think so?" Anais asked.

Lyssa nodded.

"Alright. I'll do it. Let's make sure the others are on board first, though. I don't want to blindside them with my leaving." Anais bit her bottom lip. "I also want to wait until Drin leaves, for sure."

"Of course, we wouldn't want you to lose any time with him."

Anais rolled her eyes, moving back over to the door. "You're the worst."

"Only because you know I'm right." Lyssa tapped on her computer control to bring up a new holo-display comm screen.

"I'll let you get back to it," Anais said. She departed the office and walked back through the library. People looked over at her, and Anais noticed she moved with a little bounce to her step.

She was happy. For the first time since she remembered, she had some internal peace. Whether it came from God, Drin, or the fact she finally had some useful input for her people and her world, she couldn't tell. Maybe it was all three.

Instead of taking the direct route back, Anais decided to circle around to the old pond where she'd hidden as a child, and where she and Drin had almost lost everything to the Sekaran forces.

Thin rays of sunlight beamed onto the water through the tree line, creating a heavenly scene before her. Anais breathed in the fresh air, enjoying her home planet for the first time since she could remember. The smoke smell from all of the fighting had finally died out, leaving the fresh scents of the forest, grass, and moss. Anais took it all in.

She closed her eyes and lingered for several minutes in peace, falling into meditation. Was this what it was like when Drin performed his morning prayers? It made her think she should follow his lead. *God, thank you for everything you've done for me and for my world.*

It was a simple prayer, but she opened her eyes again. Everything seemed right with her world. Some of the Templars could prattle on and on for hours when they prayed, but Anais didn't feel comfortable rambling. It felt like she was wasting God's time if she told Him more than what was necessary.

For a long time, she hadn't been certain whether God existed, but after all of the miracles she'd seen, and the ones she'd been able to perform herself, she couldn't doubt the existence of a supreme being watching over her. She hoped without Drin present, God would continue to bless her. Drin was faithful to a fault, and Anais still wasn't sure where she fit in the divine plan.

All she could do was work her hardest. Determined, she circled the pond and headed back to her residence. She had a trip to plan, and for the first time in a long time, she had to do it alone, without her favorite Templar helping her.

THREE

Drin fell into line in the *Justicar's* briefing room. His Templar brothers stood on either side, in front, and behind him, over a hundred warriors in total. Baifed was to his immediate left, but to his right, where his good friend Jellal used to stand in formation, was a new soldier, Marque.

Though Drin had no problem with Marque, it wasn't the same. He missed Jellal. Life among the Templars wouldn't be the same without him. Such was the cost of war.

Commander Shayne paced the front of the line, ensuring everyone was in proper order, inspecting his men. Everyone stood at attention, nanites forming their base armor, no helmet, as was proper procedure for these briefings. Shayne made no comment, as the Templars were a well-trained force. No one would dare be out of compliance.

Drin couldn't help but feel uncomfortable in the line of soldiers. Heat radiated from the sheer number of bodies packed into the room, blasting into his face, though his nanites regulated his internal temperature. He'd stood here hundreds of times. More than heat caused his discomfort now.

He'd been so used to working alone, or in a small group. From his liberation of Altequine, to restoring Deklyn with his friends, he'd been in a position of leadership or solo. Those missions had gone well, and Drin found he enjoyed the autonomy he'd been provided these last months.

Independence had never been a permanent situation. Drin understood he would have to return to his duties on the *Justicar*, but time passed so quickly. Battle after battle had kept him occupied, which hadn't given him much time to reflect on what he'd been doing as he'd wanted to accomplish when he first left his people. Regardless, his relationship was different with the others now. He couldn't be sure he would ever fit in.

No one treated him poorly, but his absence from his brothers had created an irreparable rift. He couldn't quite place it. The way the other men laughed together, or seemed to choose to speak to others first, even though Drin had lived with them since they arrived on Deklyn—he couldn't help but feel some separation.

Scripture didn't give him any consolation on the matter. Lord Yezuah maintained perfect fellowship with his battle leaders when he had come to Eloria. He never wavered in his loyalty, never faltered. Not that Drin did either, but he wished he found a verse or passage in the Holy Book that would clearly tell him what his path should be to restore the unity he once felt with his brothers.

Father Cline entered the room. The Templars pushed their feet together, creating a loud *clap* sound in the room. It snapped Drin from his thoughts as he focused on the elder priest, whose brown robes flowed behind him. Cline approached a dais at the front of the room and lifted his hand in the air. The sleeves of his robes fell back from where they had covered his hands as he lifted them. "Good afternoon," he said.

"Good afternoon, Father," the Templars said in unison.

"May you find peace in all your endeavors," he said.

"And to you as well," the Templars said.

"We've gathered here today in service of our Lord Yezuah, may he reign in heaven and in this universe forever, so we might further his kingdom and do glory to his name. We will soon be embarking upon a journey that, Yezuah willing, could reshape the balance of power in the galaxy, the details of which I'll be briefing you on shortly." He paused, surveying everyone present. "But first, let us pray."

The Templars bowed their heads. Drin watched but dropped his head a moment afterward, closing his eyes.

"O, Great Architect, designer of all we see," Father Cline said, "watch over us now as we embark upon your holy mission, keep us safe from enemy harm, and allow us to be beacons of light amongst the darkness of space, that we may guide worlds toward you and your eternal kingdom. Help us to remain focused as we receive the intelligence briefing, so we might be able to put the information to use for your righteous cause. Be with us now and through the last battle to eternity, forever and ever, amen."

"Amen," the Templars repeated.

Drin lifted his head to see a large, translucent holo-display activate behind Father Cline. It showed a gray world, with large ice caps taking up at least two-thirds of the planet, with a small center band that looked to be inhabitable.

"Behind me is Jaynen's World, named for the explorer who colonized it in the year of our Lord three hundred and fifteen, and set up a mining colony along the equatorial region. The world has been behind Sekaran lines for the last two hundred years, deep within our enemy's territory.

"Several months ago, the church uncovered information of a Sekaran weapon being developed, which could open a black hole in the center of worlds, devouring entire planets. If the weapon were deployed, it could cause entire systems to fall to their tyranny from the threat of its use."

Father Cline paced to the other side of the display. The three-dimensional image shifted, zooming in on an area in the equatorial region, a mountain range, which had several large openings for miners to enter, and tracks protruding from it to carry the ore away to different cities.

"Our intelligence agents have tracked the weapon to this location on Jaynen's World. It's being constructed underground. We believe that in three weeks' time, the Sekarans will be unveiling the weapon and deploying it for a first test-run. We want to intercept and destroy this weapon before they can deploy it," he said.

The Templars muttered amongst themselves. Marque frowned. "Heading into their territory would require a full-frontal assault," he muttered.

Father Cline held up his hands. "I understand your misgivings. A battle for this planet will be a costly one. We've already lost scores of intelligence agents as they obtained information about this superweapon over the past several months. Their sacrifices will be remembered, and we must make sure they are not in vain. Therefore, the *Justicar* will be joining our main fleet to make a push toward Jaynen's world. There will be a major confrontation with the bulk of the Sekaran fleet, but if just a few of us get through to be able to remove this weapon of mass destruction from the universe at large, the cost will be worth it. We cannot allow the Sekarans to have this kind of power."

Father Cline paused and glanced amongst the assembled Templars. "Are there any questions?"

Marque cleared his throat. "Yes. Do the Sekarans have a large force present at the world already? Is that why we're bringing a whole fleet?"

"There will be robust defenses," Father Cline said, "but we believe the Sekarans will bring in their reinforcements once we take the world. The fleet will be there for defense so we can have time to secure the weapon and destroy it."

"How many troop carriers will be joining us?" Commander Shane asked.

"Ten," Father Cline said.

The answer caused rumbles among the ranks. Ten was more than a lot, it was a fifth of the fleet. The Cardinals must be very concerned about this superweapon, much more than normal targets. If the battle were as large as they anticipated, this would be the biggest battle the Templars had faced in more than a hundred years. A decisive victory or loss with that size of a fleet alone could change the course of power in the galaxy.

Drin shifted his weight to one foot, finding the whole scope of the mission to be uncomfortable. The pressure mounted on him like a weight pressing down upon his shoulders. The Sekarans having a superweapon was a dire situation, but such a large battle would put much at stake.

"Who's going to be sent to secure the weapon on the planet?" Baifed asked.

It was the most important question that could have been asked. The room fell silent as all of the Templars wanted to learn the answer.

"I will be meeting with unit commanders separately to discuss assignments. No matter what your role, you will be important. The Templars will lead the way for the rest of our units, and I am honored to serve the Lord with all of you." He clasped his hands together. "We'll be departing tomorrow. Please, get everything in order and make sure you are well rested tonight. We will have a prayer service at sunset. Thank you, and God bless all of you. Power and glory to Yezuah!"

"Power and glory to Yezuah!" the Templars echoed.

Everyone disbursed, some engaged in conversations but most heading toward the bottleneck of the doorway into the main corridors of the *Justicar*. Being in the center of the room, it took Drin some time to find his way out of the room. He had a bad feeling about this mission, something he couldn't quite place. It loomed over him, and he knew from his own habits that it wouldn't go away any time soon.

When he finally reached the corridor, he moved toward the Templar sleeping quarters, a long room stacked with double-bunked beds, with small drawers on the side. Templars were not encouraged to keep possessions, and Drin had none other than his Holy Book, a datapad, his hygiene supplies, and his pillow. The nanites created all of the clothes he needed. He could conjure them as the situation warranted.

Several others were in the room as well, relaxing in between training sessions, meals, or their shifts on the ship. All green-faced Elorians like Drin, black hair of various lengths. Drin kept his short for ease's sake, but others liked longer, braided hair, like several of the heroes of ancient times.

One person varied in tone from the others in the room, the purple-skinned, six-armed Skree, Err-dio, who entered the large chambers, eyes searching.

"Looking for me?" Drin asked, waving him over.

"I am," Err-dio said, bounding toward him. "Is there anything I can assist you with?"

Drin frowned. "Not at the moment. Father Cline says we'll be deploying for battle soon."

"I heard some others talking about it. Sounds like a big one? Usually the Templars are jovial when they go into battle... now..." He shook his head. "The mood is a nervous one."

"For good reason," Drin said.

Err-dio frowned. "I don't suppose there's anything that could lighten the mood?"

"No, somberness is appropriate." Drin had wanted time to think, and having someone by him made it near-impossible. Only a day until they'd be departing. It meant he didn't have much time to speak with Anais. No, he should probably not go see her at all.

The last thing he needed was a head full of sinful desires before heading on a mission of this import. He should be away from her.

But he worried about her. She tended to get herself into trouble without him, and the thought of her in danger made Drin much more agitated than the prospect of dying in a tense battle. He wouldn't be able to sleep with her occupying his mind.

"Perhaps there is something you can do for me."

Err-dio's eyes lit up. "Yes?"

"You're not going to like it," Drin said. Err-dio wanted to tail him, to train with Drin in combat, and to serve him as a squire. Drin could use his ambition here, but he felt bad doing so since he knew it wouldn't be what the Skree desired.

"I am here to serve the Lord, however I may."

"I want you to stay on Deklyn and watch over Anais," Drin said. He wasn't used to giving these kind of orders—it was something Father Cline or Commander Shayne would do. Something uncomfortable, against the will of the person receiving the orders, but for the better of all. Would Err-dio accept?

The Skree's eyes searched Drin, his expression flat. He couldn't have been pleased, but he nodded nonetheless. "Of course. I see the wisdom in the task. I will do my best to keep her safe, so help me God."

Drin extended a hand. "You're a good man, Err-dio. If I don't see you again, it was a pleasure serving with you."

"I wish you wouldn't speak like that. But if the worst occurs, we will meet again in Yezuah's kingdom, yes?" Err-dio clasped Drin's hand.

FOUR

A SHADOW FELL OVER THE ALREADY SHADY FOREST CITY. THE Elorian warship rose from the spaceport, blocking out the sun as it ascended into the atmosphere. It left Anais with a sense of emptiness. It was as if someone ripped her heart from her chest and threw it into the atmosphere with the ship.

Her lip quivered, but she bit down on it. She wouldn't break into tears. This wouldn't be the end. She would see Drin again.

Even though she tried to will the outcome, part of her doubted her assessment. Either way, she didn't like being apart from him.

She slumped into one of the iron lawn chairs out back of her mansion. Such a big house, now rebuilt, and even with her servants and guards, she couldn't have imagined a lonelier place. She wished she had taken off with the Elorians, but she had spoken with Father Cline a week prior, and they both had agreed her place was here with her people.

Anais sighed.

"Everything okay?" came a male voice from behind her.

Anais stretched to glance behind her. Elaym stood there, a brown-furred man. His coat started to shine more than it had in recent weeks, as he slowly recovered from the torture and malnutrition he suffered under Sekaran capture. "Yeah, just a lot of stress lately," she said, pushing herself back up out of the chair to turn to greet him.

Elaym gave Anais a warm hug. "Good. I can't even imagine what it must be like, having those Elorian machines in your bloodstream. There's rumors that they mind-control you."

"It's not like that," Anais said. "They're there, and they can feel me...but I'm pretty sure I control them." Did she? She'd never considered the possibility that their presence in her system might influence her in the same way she directed the nanites.

"I believe you," Elaym said, pulling back from her. "You wanted to see me?"

"Yeah, I want to talk about the trip."

"Right. You're going to head to Parthenon Station to try to rebuild some of our former alliances, right?"

Anais nodded. "It's more than that, though. I thought about it, and I'm going to need some help. I shouldn't go alone. I know the other Merchant Lords are extremely busy, but I don't know who else I can trust with our plant's future."

Elaym nodded. "Lyssa's got me tasked with building our planetary defenses. Our parents were lazy about it before, and it allowed the Sekarans to sneak through and gain control. We don't want that to happen again. I don't know if I should go off-world."

"I thought about that," Anais said. "Nagell is the one who introduced us to the Sagitar Mercenaries who helped us liberate the world. I'm sure he can help with defense systems and other equipment. It might even be a good idea to have a retainer contract with a mercenary group like the Sagitar so they can come to our aide if we ever have another crisis."

Elaym's ears twitched to his side, something Anais noticed he did when he contemplated. "That's not a half-bad idea." He chuckled. "Are you sure you don't want to take over the defense planning?"

"I've got enough on my plate with this," Anais said. "But I really want you to come with me. I've already run it by Lyssa this morning. At first, she balked at the idea, but she sees the merit in having two representatives. If I get sick, or something happens, you can pick up the slack on my end, or vice versa. It's important."

"Well, when you put it that way," Elaym said.

"You'll go?" Anais smiled at him.

"Yeah, I don't see why not. I've always wanted to go off-world. Never had the chance."

"Great!"

Someone rounded the corner of the mansion to the backyard. Anais recognized him as her six-armed Skree friend.

"Anais!" Err-dio's tone was bright, as it usually was. The Skree had been so grateful for their world being liberated—they'd been subjugated for so long, freedom meant everything to them. The entire race proclaimed the Elorian religion as their official one. Drin had converted an entire world with little effort. Well, a lot of effort, but not in the preaching sense.

"Shouldn't you be off with the Elorian ship?" Anais asked, pointing skyward.

"That's what I came to talk to you about." The Skree clasped hands with Elaym when he greeted them. "Hello, Elaym."

"Afternoon," Elaym said.

Err-dio turned to Anais. "Drin left me on the planet with instructions to follow you. I'm to act as your squire while he is away."

"My squire?" Anais asked, taken aback. "I'm not really a Templar."

"You have the gift of Yezuah inside of you."

The nanites. The Elorians revered them religiously, and Anais had to admit she had a sixth sense about her, for a lack of a better term. "Well, I won't turn down the help. I was just telling Elaym I'm planning an expedition back to Parthenon Station."

"Is that safe?" Err-dio asked.

"Is anything?" Anais shrugged. "It needs to be done, and I'm the only one other than Lyssa who Nagell might listen to and try to help."

Err-dio nodded. "If that's where you're going, I will come with you and guard you faithfully."

"Thanks. We could use the help." She glanced at Elaym. "I think we should both bring a few people with us. There is safety in numbers, and though Nagell leads Parthenon Station and is friendly, it's a large place. Anything can happen."

"Agreed," Elaym said. "I'll bring two of my retainers."

"I'll find a couple of my house servants to join us, as well," Anais said. She glanced between the men. "Looks like we have a plan. How about this? We'll leave in three days. It'll give you time to settle anything you have outstanding and delegate your duties to someone else."

"Sounds good," Elaym said.

"Great. I'll meet you at the spaceport then." Even though she felt empty without Drin, having a purpose helped matters. If she could stay focused on her world, she could forget about him more easily. And that's what she needed to do.

FIVE

Drin grunted, lifting a heavy barbell weight over his shoulders. His muscles flexed, able to push the weight up for his tenth repetition. Baifed kept close to him, in case he faltered, but Drin didn't require the spot.

He liked to perform his workouts without the aid of the nanites, ensuring he maximized his own potential before relying on the tiny machines. Some of the younger Templars lifted as much as they could with nanite assistance to try to appear impressive, but Drin had no need to brag about his strength. He would show what he could do on the field of battle.

He set down the weight, exhaling a deep breath, and wiping the sweat from his brow.

"I daresay you're growing stronger, brother Drin," Baifed said.

"I've been spending a lot of time training," Drin said. He moved over to the water filtration system and grabbed himself a glass, filling it, and guzzling some of the cool liquid. It felt good going down his throat, and he could sense the nanites utilizing the water to regulate his temperature.

"More than the rest of us. Are you trying to work out frustrations on your weights?" Baifed asked.

It wasn't a snide question. Baifed showed genuine concern for him. Drin appreciated the sentiment. "I don't know," he said. It was true. He didn't. He certainly had some frustrations, but there was little he could do about them. Since they had departed for Jayden's World, he'd been uneasy—with the mission, with leaving Anais and her world—and his mind reeled.

The last three nights, Drin found himself tossing and turning instead of being able to sleep. He'd hoped his hard workouts would wear him out to the point where he'd be able to sleep regardless, but it didn't seem to have any effect. Father Cline had instructed the Templars to rest, and Drin needed to. He had to be at peak performance soon enough.

"Perhaps God can show you the way," Baifed said. "Would you care to join Marque and me in prayer?"

Drin nodded. "I'll meet you in the chapel after getting cleaned up."

They departed each other's company, and Drin made directly for the sonic shower system. The shower removed all of the sweat and toxins freed from his skin, and then he summoned his nanites to make formal prayer robes and headed to the chapel.

At least a dozen Templars graced the pews, kneeling before the altar at the front of the room. Father Cline knelt at the dais, beads in his hands, muttering repetitions of the Lord's Prayer and Marayh's Lament. Drin found Baifed and Marque, knelt beside them and began his own repetition of prayers.

There was something calming in the prayers, the way he knew them so intimately that the uttering of them was a rote task. He didn't need to think, other than to focus and keep his place. He could just repeat the words. It calmed Drin's mind for those few brief moments. The Lord brought him peace, as he'd desired.

After a half hour of prayer, Drin and the others stood and left the room. Father Cline followed behind in the corridors. He caught up to the Templars. "My children, we'll be reaching Jayden's World in three hours. Report to Commander Shayne in the shuttle bay. You'll need to be at the ready to deploy immediately."

"Yes, Father," Baifed said for them.

"And there's something further you should know. Two hours ago, I received a communique from Nita IV. The Sekarans engaged in a surprise attack with a massive assault. They brought four of their dreadnought ships."

Drin tried to keep the panic off his face. Nita IV was one of the Elorians' most populated worlds. The Sekarans moving there was troubling. Had they found out about the Elorian ship movements and planned a counter assault? Their fleet admiral had strategic sense if this had been planned. The movement of so many troop carriers left the Elorians vulnerable in several areas.

"The Church decided to divert nine of our ten carriers to make a show of overwhelming force," Father Cline said. "If the Sekarans moved such a fleet, we've determined Jayden's World cannot be that well-fortified. The *Justicar* will be moving on the offensive alone, and we anticipate we will be able to secure the world while the others defend Nita IV. We can strike a blow and defend our world simultaneously."

Drin nodded. It wasn't ideal, but they would manage. It meant the Templars on the *Justicar* would be the front lines of assault at Jayden's World. He only hoped the cardinals had not underestimated the Sekaran military presence there. They usually had the right of things, and Elorian intelligence was second to none, but they still erred from time to time, as all people did.

"The Lord will watch over us and provide," Baifed said.

"Indeed, He will, my son," Father Cline said. They reached the bank of lifts. "I must depart for the bridge. Yezuah be with you."

"And you," Marque said.

The three Templars took the lift down to the shuttle bay as Father Cline had instructed them. They found several hundred other Templars and regular pilots there already. The ship's complement was ready for mobilization.

The Templars fell into line with their unit. A large holo-display on the back wall showed a map of the *Justicar's* progress through space, as well as the blurred stars of hyperspace travel from the ship's exterior camera.

Shane walked the line. "Are you all ready for battle?"

"Aye, sir!" the Templars said in unison.

"Will you give your all for the Lord our God and His people?"

"Aye, sir!"

"Will you defeat the Sekaran heretics and bring peace to the galaxy?"

"Aye, sir!" The third cheer was the loudest of all. The feeling of unity made the hair on Drin's neck stand. Togetherness. Frater-nity. They were the Templars, and they would not fail.

"Good," Shayne said, stopping in front of Drin. "We're going to split our team—half into vipers and half into drop ships. Drin, Baifed, Marque, Hulius, and Matrin, you'll be with me in the vipers. The rest of you head for dropship delta. There's still some time before we arrive, but we need to be ready to go on a moment's notice."

"Yes, sir!" the Templars said.

"Go!" Shayne said, clapping his hands.

The Templars scrambled for their different positions. Drin jogged to his viper, changing his nanite attire to his flight gear. He didn't form a helmet yet, as he wouldn't need to be confined in such a space until he was ready to fly. Technicians serviced his viper, topping off the fuel and inspecting the ship in case of any last-minute deficiencies. They found none and moved to the next, leaving Drin alone with his ship.

Drin placed his hand on the nose of the viper. Even though it was a machine, he loved his ship. It might have been foolish, but he'd been through so much in the vessel. He was attached to it.

They were supposed to disavow all attachments, but Drin figured he could have the one. He used his viper in service of the Lord, after all. Didn't he?

He also had an attachment to Anais. Why couldn't he stop thinking of that blasted girl? He shook his head.

Time passed slowly as he waited in anticipation. He ran through various potential outcomes in his head, from an easy victory to the doomsday scenario where the Sekarans overwhelmed them. He prayed the latter wouldn't happen. It couldn't happen. The Templars were God's faithful.

He had to remain calm. Fighting in a frenzy would do no good. Focus, keeping an empty mind—that was how one performed best in battle. Even with the awareness, Drin couldn't stop himself from becoming on edge. Too much rode on the line here. The atmosphere in the shuttle bay didn't help, with hundreds of soldiers primed for battle. It felt electric, for lack of a better term.

The ship lurched ever so slightly as they dropped out of hyperspace. Drin climbed the ladder to his cockpit, in case he had to do a hard launch immediately, but he stopped at the top rung to look back at the holo-display in the back corner.

"What in God's name?" one of the technicians said.

Several mutters followed from below. Drin narrowed his eyes at the scene on the screen.

It was the planet, just like in the briefing display. But there were no Sekaran warships present. The planet was almost unoccupied. It was completely quiet. A few satellites circled the moon, and Drin spotted the orbital defense systems, which weren't active as of yet. They were out of range still.

"Let's move!" Drin heard Shayne shouting.

Drin hopped into the cockpit and secured himself, clicking his safety belt together. He concentrated on forming a nanite helmet and visor, a translucent tactical display shimmering into form. The top of the cockpit slid forward, sealing him into his viper. His breaths made an ominous noise within the visor, his senses amplified within the confined space, but it was a situation he'd been in dozens of times before. Nothing could prevent him from being ready.

According to the holo-map, the *Justicar* arrived at its planned coordinates.

"Viper pilots, ready for launch," the flight deck controller said through the comm.

Drin powered up his viper engines and readied himself. He would be the third out of the bay, behind Commander Shayne and Baifed. The more senior officers went first, and Drin, despite his unorthodox work over the last several months, had gained seniority. Pride swelled within him as his engines flared and his viper sailed out of the bay and into space.

He banked to the right, following his commander, and Jayden's World appeared in front of them. The brown world with the giant ice caps slowly filled Drin's entire vision. He was prepared to do some battle, but the orbital defenses didn't blast at them. What was going on?

"It's too quiet," Baifed said through his comm.

"I agree," Commander Shayne said. "Let's see what we encounter once we drop into the atmosphere."

A dozen vipers flew into a V formation, headed by Commander Shayne. They dropped into Jayden's World's thin air in unison, computer piloting adjusting their entry angles so they wouldn't burn up in the atmosphere.

Soon, they flew along the clouds of the world and descended below the puffy forms. Drin spotted a few settlements below, but he couldn't see much activity from his vantage. Everything seemed so dead. Had the Sekarans already ravaged the world and departed?

"Our landing point is ahead. My scanners aren't showing any life signs," Commander Shayne said.

The vipers continued their descent, flying low above the hills and giant rocks, but not so low they would be at risk of colliding with them. The winds were strong on this world, but Drin could handle it with his piloting capabilities.

Shayne set down at a long strip to the south of twin mountains. Drin landed behind his commander, noting the scenery around them. His nanites zoomed in on the mountain, allowing Drin to see several cave entrances, along with tracks for vehicles and equipment to travel in and out of them. This had been a robust mining world at one point. But why were no people present?

The Templars opened their cockpits and jumped to the ground. They met together, Shayne holding an electronic scanner as he surveyed the area. "Still no signs of life," Shayne said. "I'd think it was some sort of masking field interfering with our equipment if I didn't see how dead this world was with my own eyes."

"Where could everyone have gone?" Baifed asked.

Drin turned toward the caves and took some steps away from his companions. Mining equipment still lined the hills, along with other vehicles. They looked as if they had been abandoned quickly. "I think the Sekarans were aware of our planned assault on this planet and reacted accordingly," Drin said.

"Could be," Shayne said, stepping to his side. "But why wouldn't they just bring a fleet here to take us on? It's not like the Sekarans to run from a fight."

It was true. Their enemy prided themselves on fighting to the death. They didn't run even in the direst of circumstances. Drin had regretted having to kill several Sekaran soldiers when they had no chance in a battle, but nothing he did ever caused them to waver. Their bravery was admirable.

"There's no one here. I would lay odds on their weapon no longer being present, as well," Baifed said.

"We still need to head to the caves and investigate to be sure," Shayne said. He motioned for the others to follow him.

Drin took ten paces toward the cave structures when his comm line beeped. An incoming message from the *Justicar*, Priority Level One.

Shayne answered. "Commander Shayne here. We're receiving your transmission, *Justicar*."

"Templars, this is Father Cline." The message rang through in all of their helmets. "We're showing a huge energy build-up in the cave formations ahead of you. It's growing, and we believe an explosion is imminent. Return to your vipers and launch immediately."

Shayne stopped and turned. "You heard the Father. Let's go, go, go!" he commanded in his gruff tone.

Drin turned back to his ship and jogged toward it. He couldn't linger with the warning the *Justicar* had given them. If they were worried about an explosion where their vipers were parked, it must have been a large energy build-up, as the caves were not situated all that close to them. It would have been a ten or fifteen-minute walk at the least, from what Drin could ascertain.

He quickly climbed the rungs into his cockpit and sealed it. Shayne and Baifed had barely beaten him to theirs, firing up their engines and taking off, leaving a cloud of dust in front of Drin's viper. Several pebbles hit his ship's shielding, causing energy to flicker around the ship.

Drin fired his engines, taking off in a steep ascent toward the sky. He pushed the ship hard, gravity pinning him back against his seat. He was glad he had the nanite aiding his physiology or he might have blacked out from the stress of the maneuver.

The quick takeoff proved vital. A rumbling came from below, which Drin at first thought was a sound from his thrusters straining themselves. Looking back over his shoulder, he saw a dust cloud rising and spreading, waves of dirt and debris looking like the ocean as it plumed outward and upward.

The force of the blast rocked the viper, Drin barely able to compensate to keep flying straight. Debris caught up with the ship as he flew further past the atmosphere. Rocks and specks of dust pelted into the vessel. How could so much energy have come from the dead world? What happened down there?

He rose, brown dust covering the view around him. Drin cranked his thrusters to the limits. They redlined, and the visor in front of him warned him he was going too hard. He could keep it up for another few seconds before his engines would fail, and so he did.

His ship barely kept ahead of the growing cloud of dust, and he broke through the atmosphere into the darkness of space. Several of his companions' ships flew around him, but a quick scan of his monitor showed four vipers had failed to make it out of the smoke in time.

Drin banked to the side so he could get a view of whatever had happened, expecting to see the area he'd just left plumed into a mushroom cloud explosion.

Instead, the entire planet had crumbled into debris. Where the ice caps had been was a full cloud of smoke. The world had crumpled like caked dirt smashing against pavement. Large pieces of the planet floated in space, its hot magma core brightening the area.

Jayden's World had been destroyed.

The sight was shocking, but the implications were worse. The Sekarans hadn't merely been working on a superweapon that could destroy worlds—they had completed it, and the Templars had fallen right into their trap.

SIX

ANAIS HUNG OVER THE OPENING INTO THE COCKPIT OF THE transport shuttle as Elaym's house guard flew them toward the cylindrical metal station—their destination. She'd thought they might have to expend considerable effort in finding a pilot, but Elaym's man turned out to be very competent. His name was Blaque, and he'd run shipping routes on behalf of Elaym's family for two decades.

The pilot's fur was a dirty-white color and even seated, he was about as tall as Anais. He stayed locked on the controls.

"Parthenon Station to Deklyn ambassadorial. You are cleared for landing in shuttle bay three-two-three," said a voice through the comm. "Please turn over controls to our AI, and we will have auto-pilot guide you in."

Blaque set the controls to auto and sat back. "I hate this part. I don't like trusting computers."

"I've never seen a problem," Anais said.

Blaque laughed. "Because you haven't been around many trade operations. Accidents happen all the time."

The ship was grabbed by a tractor beam and brought into the

landing bay. Despite Blaque's reservations, everything went smoothly. The ship landed without any incident, and the back ramp dropped into the bay.

Anais recalled the last time they were here, with no preparation and no advance calls. They'd almost gotten stuck in the station with no way out. This time, she'd made sure to call ahead and ensure she had a meeting with the station CEO Nagell before they arrived.

A station ops crew was there to greet them, taking their bags and escorting them to guest quarters to drop off their things and refresh themselves before the meeting. Anais appreciated being able to sprawl out on a comfortable bed after the journey cooped up inside the transport, even if it was only for a few minutes.

Once she showered and slipped into a fresh change of clothes, she met Elaym and Err-dio in the hallway, along with their retainers, and made their way to the station's premier conference room.

Waiters attended them when they entered, offering a variety of small plates from different systems, showing off the reach of Parthenon Station and how much business they were able to do. Anais's stomach growled, and she helped herself to several of the samples. The servers also offered alcohol, which Elaym took, but Anais refrained from. She drank in her prior life, but something didn't feel right about consuming alcohol when she had the Elorian nanites inside of her. The Holy Book said the body was a gift from God, and to treat it as one would a prized offering. It didn't explicitly say to abstain, and Anais had seen the Templars drinking after some of their battles, but for her, it seemed best.

After they'd relaxed for several minutes—no doubt an important negotiation tactic Nagell used on his guests to soften them prior to meeting—the station's CEO finally arrived. Nagell stood, a flat face with a black, wet nose and a furred physique. In a universe with so many different species, any similarities put Anais more at home. It was probably why her world did so much business with Parthenon Station.

"Greetings," Nagell said. "Welcome back, and also I must congratulate you on reclaiming your world. That was no small task, even with the help of the Sagitar Mercenaries. Did I not tell you they were the best?" He grabbed a glass of a bubbly, red liquid.

Anais stepped forward and gave Nagell a handshake. "Thank you. Allow me to introduce my fellow Merchant Lord, Elaym. You've met my Skree friend, Err-dio," Anais said, motioning to the others. She didn't bother to introduce the rest of her party, as they wouldn't be part of the negotiations.

Nagell shook the other two men's hands. "A pleasure to meet you, I'm sure." He reclined into a seat at the end of the conference table.

Anais and her people took chairs surrounding him. She swiveled in her chair to face Nagell. "I appreciate all the accommodations you've provided us. We might be set up here for some time. Like I told you in the comm, our world has very little commerce flowing to and from it since the Sekaran invasion. I need to jump-start the trade economy and get my world working again on the galactic stage."

Nagell slurped his drink and set it down. "I understand. We engaged in much profitable trade with your father for many years. But...I'm afraid I'm going to have to deliver bad news for you. I'm happy to host you here on the station, but I'm afraid I can't risk Parthenon's neutrality in the conflict between the two rival religions. It's bad for business, you see. If one of those empires turns on us, we could very well find ourselves in a predicament similar to the one you're in now. I can't allow that with the fiduciary responsibility I have to the residents, employees, and investors here. You understand?"

Anais tried to keep her expression neutral, though it became difficult to hide her disappointment. She couldn't relent here, not just because of some words. Nagell negotiated for a living, it's what he did. She had to come back with an offer, right? "I don't. We've had trade agreements in the past, and I think—I mean, I *know*—we can have a profitable relationship in the future. Nagell, you've been great to my family in the past, I'd love to continue our working relationship."

Nagell stood. "I'm happy to allow you use of our station while you're in this sector. We're officially neutral, and using our ports is something anyone can do, barring criminals, but I can't get involved in your world's dealings at this time. It's too hot. I really wish I could help you more. I do like you. This isn't personal."

Anais stood along with him. "Then help me again. Point me to a world where we can open trade. We need your help just as badly as when you gave us information on the mercenaries. You got involved then, didn't you?"

"The situation escalated when the Elorians came to your world directly. The perception of my involvement in your governmental affairs could cause all sorts of rumors. I can't take the risk. I'm sorry, Anais, but the decision is final."

Anger welled in her. Anais banged her fist on the conference table. It rattled, causing everyone present to turn their attentions to her in surprise.

She had gone through so much because of the Sekarans, and they kept haunting her in more ways than she could fathom. It didn't even make sense to her. If word got out she was on the station, wouldn't it be enough to draw their ire? She couldn't say she understood politics very well. She'd never had to do much other than look pretty when she was younger. But she didn't want to push the situation, lest she and the others be kicked out of their accommodations.

"Nagell, thank you for the help you've given us," Anais said, having to bite her tongue. It would do no good to lash out at him. She didn't want to turn Parthenon Station into an enemy when they were friendly to her, even if they weren't willing to provide help.

Nagell inclined his head. Something shifted in his eyes, but Anais couldn't tell what it meant with the species. Was it regret? It would have been if she had seen the look in the face of a Deklyn. "Thank you for understanding. Now please, enjoy the rest of your stay on the station." He motioned to the door.

Anais led the way, with Elaym and the others right behind her. They shuffled out of the conference room. She wasn't sure where to go, but she didn't want to go back to her quarters and brood. "Let's find a bar or something," Anais said.

"I can agree with that. What just happened in there?" Elaym said.

"It looks like Nagell's running scared," Anais said after glancing back over her shoulder to make sure he wasn't still in earshot. "I don't blame them, I suppose. It's not very fun to be wrapped up in the Sekarans' attentions."

"True," Elaym said.

"If no one is willing to fight, however, doesn't it allow evil to win by proxy?" Err-dio asked.

"Yes, but you have to go through certain experiences to know stepping aside for evil is evil. We can't blame them for their inaction. They're not at fault. It does leave us back at square one, though. We need to regroup and figure out what we can do, because we can't go home empty-handed."

They wound around corridors until they found someone who appeared like they worked for the station, as he wore a green jumpsuit with a badge of a logo often seen in the corridors of Parthenon Station. A brief conversation later, and Anais had been pointed to the station's most popular transient lounge, a place with a robust menu of foods that ranged dozens of star systems and, of course, libations to match.

The lounge had a red theme to it, with dark burgundy cushions, lighting that shone red, and countertops of a maroon marble substance. Soft, strange music with a droning beat played in the background and dozens of patrons of what seemed to be just as many species packed into the place. There was an AI attendant at the front of the lounge where guests checked in. Anais told the attendant the number of her party, and they waited for a table.

With their followers, they had a slightly larger group than would fit at most tables. The staff would have to combine two tables together. She didn't mind waiting, though she wished she had a better idea of what to say to the others. The rest of her group dragged their feet, eyes cast downward, ears drooping. The reality of their situation in which Deklyn would have no help from the station was setting in.

They couldn't give up. Her people depended on them.

Anais' name was called, and a server showed them to their table. They sat and ordered, but there wasn't much of the jovial talk they'd had before the meeting with Nagell.

Anais wasn't going to partake in alcohol, so she ordered herself a hot tea. The others weren't conservative in their choices. Surprisingly, Err-dio ordered the strongest drink of anyone—a Viridian Black Tsengu, a syrup-textured drink that would have knocked Anais flat on her back.

"All right," Anais said after the waiter left. "We need ideas. Does anyone have contacts with representatives of any worlds beyond here?"

Err-dio raised three of his hands. "Sao-rin will trade with your world. He owes you a debt."

He referred to the king of the Skree. Anais nodded. At least they could get one trade deal going. The problem was, Konsin II didn't have many resources, and was in dire straits just like Deklyn. They could help marginally, but it wouldn't uplift either world, as they both needed similar materials and energy to reconstruct their ravaged cities and to build infrastructure. They needed more of a patron than a trading partner. Someone who understood there would be value later by investing in them now.

"That's a start," Anais said, not wanting to break morale further. "If you can get your king on the comm later, we can at least open up one trade route. But we're going to need a lot more if we're going to jumpstart a whole economy to get working again."

The others didn't have ideas. Blank stares and shrugs met Anais's glances, even from Elaym, who had about the same experiences in life Anais did before she was plucked from the world. None of them had any contacts worth speaking of.

The server returned with drinks, and the others appeared to be relieved to have something to do other than have Anais glare at them. She allowed the conversation to relax. Maybe when they were a little more lubricated, they would have better ideas. She wished Elaym would have been more useful. His lack of ambition made her want to shake some sense into him. He looked like he wanted to go home and forget about this whole trip.

A lanky creature, one who stood about twice as tall as Anais, and with a long, flowing brown coat over a scraggly-haired body approached the table. "I couldn't help but overhear your conversation. Forgive me, I was not eavesdropping, but my race has sensitive hearing."

"As does ours," Elaym said, looking up.

"My name is Cohn. I'm a trader captain with a fairly sizable ship. What are you looking for with your world? And where are you from?" He cocked his head. "I don't think I've seen your species before."

"We're Deklyn," Anais said.

"Wood exporters?"

Anais nodded. "You know us."

"I think some of the trim in my cockpit is made from your trees. Fine quality timber."

"We try to produce the best," Anais said.

"Mind if I join you?"

The others slid over for Cohn to be able to pull up a chair at the end. He sat, stretching his long legs off to the side.

"So you've got a ship. Do you represent your world? Can we meet with any of the officials?" Anais asked.

"One thing at a time," Cohn said. "Have you tried to meet with station heads? They're accommodating in pointing people in the right direction."

"We did," Elaym said. "They didn't want to help us."

Anais wished he hadn't volunteered the information. It was important to play everything they could close to the vest. She didn't know this Cohn from anyone else here. He could have been fishing for information for all kinds of reasons.

"That's a shame," Cohn said. "Why?"

"Ah, that was private information," Anais said hurriedly, trying to get the words in before Elaym could speak again.

"I understand, matters of state. I'll tell you what. I know a number of people here on the station who are gathering together. It's a little dangerous, though. Not that these are bad people. No one's selling narcotics or weapons or anything that would be illegal in most systems, but these worlds were attacked by Sekarans. They're trying to rebuild together and need more help."

"We were attacked by Sekarans, too," Elaym said.

Anais really wanted to put a gag in him. She tried not to let her annoyance show.

"Is that so?" Cohn said. "Well, this might be good fortune for all of us." He set a crystal down on the table. "My private access comm line information is on here. Call me later tonight, and I'll work on setting up a meeting for you." He stood, towering over Anais. "I should get back to my crew. Very fortuitous in meeting you here today."

"Yeah," Anais said.

Elaym beamed at the creature. He was too naive, too trusting. Didn't he know better, after how the Sekarans had treated them?

Cohn bowed his head and moved off. The others at the table seemed in better spirits. At least he'd done that for them. Could it be fortuitous? God helping them because they were faithful? Or was this all too convenient? Anais wasn't so sure she trusted this creature. But for now, she needed to coach Elaym on how not to lay everything they had out on the table. "Elaym, let's take a walk and let the others relax a bit."

"Why?" Elaym asked.

"We need to talk. Come on," Anais motioned to him and stood from her seat, leaving the others behind for the time being.

SEVEN

"Drin to *Justicar*, what in God's divine universe just happened?" Drin asked through his comm.

Debris cluttered his entire view. Pebbles, rocks, and dust all crackled against the shielding of his viper. He kept his course set forward, following Commander Shayne toward the looming capital ship ahead of them.

"There was an energy build-up. It erupted within the planet, and the whole world exploded. I've never seen anything like it," Father Cline said.

"Then their superweapon is operational," Drin said under his breath.

Silence fell over the comm. If the Sekarans could take out worlds on a whim, the entire landscape of the galaxy would change. What could the Elorians do? If they sent ground units to protect civilizations, it would do no good. They'd only cause more destruction. This was a disaster.

Drin understood why the church had attempted to move on this intel so quickly, but the problem was, the Sekarans had time to counter the Elorians' plans. They'd been ready for the Templars to arrive. It was fortunate the entire force wasn't here, as originally planned. How many other systems were in danger of Sekaran strike? What if they'd planned a counter-assault on other worlds?

If there had been doubt in Drin's mind about his mission in life, of the necessity for having to do violence in the Lord's name, it evaporated now. The enemy had become world destroyers. These were the signs the prophets warned would happen in the end times. The final battle would be near.

"Fighters, return to mothership and prepare for jump. We should fall back to the Ytor system and meet with others in the fleet," Father Cline said. "Wait a minute, we're getting more energy readings."

Drin checked his cockpit's computer screen. It wasn't like the buildup back on the planet—these were hyperspace jumps coming to their conclusions. Several large objects appeared on his scanner. They blinked red. The viper issued an immediate warning as the computer AI recognized the ships jumping into the system—Sekaran battleships.

"All hands, prepare for combat!" Father Cline shouted.

"You heard the Father," Commander Shayne said. He banked his ship in a defensive pattern, gliding in the long side of the *Justicar*.

The other templars followed, keeping within formation with Shayne. Drin took his place at the first-right wing. The *Justicar* would be launching hundreds of other fighters soon, but so would the Sekarans.

Drin narrowed his eyes on space. His nanite-visor made it possible to see clearly, even in the darkness. It tracked heat readings and a cluster of ships to his twelve o'clock.

This wouldn't be an easy battle. One Sekaran battleship was tough enough of a fight, but three left them with overwhelming odds from the start. Why hadn't Father Cline hadn't called for an immediate retreat?

But he understood. The destruction of an entire planet was something they couldn't back down from. If they did, who else would fight?

Time seemed to slow as the two groups of fighters came at each other. Those moments before action always seemed to take an eternity. No matter how many times Drin had been involved in these battles, he couldn't get over the nerves that accompanied them. His stomach seemed to turn over, hairs sticking up on his arms and neck. Jitters. What if these were the last moments he would exist in this life?

As they came closer, Commander Shayne's voice deepened as he spoke into his comm, "Lord God on high, your name is sacred forever. This kingdom is yours now, as you have gifted us, and will reign eternal until you return. Forgive us our sins, as we forgive the sins of our enemies. Never let your flock go astray, but keep us apart from evil, that we may grow in our faithfulness. Power and glory to Yezuah!"

"Power and glory to Yezuah!" the others shouted.

Every time the Lord's Prayer was uttered, it brought Drin a renewed sense of hope and purpose. It energized him, as it did his brothers. His doubts evaporated. What did it matter if this life were shortened? The Lord would provide for them in His kingdom.

Drin gripped the targeting controls of his laser-repeaters. If this were going to be his final battle, he would do the Lord honor.

"Here we go," Baifed said. "Let's send those infidels straight to the Dark One's pit!"

As they came closer, the blob of heat signatures showing on his visor became clear. It was a full wall of Sekaran fighters. "Don't wait until you get into lock range. They're everywhere! Fire!" Drin shouted.

Laser-repeater bolts blasted from his ship and from the others.

The Sekarans returned fire. The darkness of space lit up into a spectacle of fireworks at once.

It was nearly impossible to tell whose shots were whose. It would make for some interesting debates over kills if they made it back to the shuttle bay of the *Justicar*. The Templars enjoyed boasting about outdoing each other in battle. There had to be some levity in the difficulties of war.

Several Sekaran ships were blasted into bits. There were so many of them, it was almost as if the laser fire couldn't miss the targets. Drin pressed forward all the same. They would do the most damage if they could get behind the lines.

He tried not to focus on the others, though from his readings, it appeared as if the Sekarans managed to take out two of the Templar fighters. He couldn't think about more of his brothers' deaths, not now. He had a job to do.

More of Drin's blasts connected against the wall of Sekaran fighters. He approached quickly as the battle erupted, and soon, he found himself having to maneuver his viper to not crash into a Sekaran vessel.

The Templars passed through the first line and through the thinner second. The overwhelming wall tactic would have worked well, but the Templars had faced it before, and they understood that breaking through and cutting holes as quickly as possible was the way to combat it. Their reinforcements would arrive from the *Justicar* soon enough, and they could flank the Sekarans during the next pass.

Once through the line and into open space again, Drin pushed his thrusters forward, then pulled back to flip his craft around. With no resistance in space, he was able to complete the somersault almost instantaneously. Without the aid of his nanites, the maneuver would have caused an ordinary pilot to blackout, but Drin had his machines to help him in all things, including this. He started firing again, picking off several Sekaran ships.

He glanced at his scanner. They had six of the original Templars from his squadron left, but they were each worth a hundred Sekarans. Vipers from the *Justicar* were en route, and the Sekaran forces were focused on the ones ahead of them. It left the rear of the Sekaran fighter wall exposed.

"Target practice, boys!" Shayne said through the comm.

The Templars fired a steady stream of laser bolts, ship after ship exploding in front of them. It was all too easy.

Until the battleships took notice of them behind the lines and started firing their much larger laser spreads.

A Templar ship exploded with one shot.

"Split up, circle around, and fall back in with our forces. They've caught on to what we're doing," Commander Shayne said.

Drin strafed to the left in his viper, keeping his forward lasers pointed toward the Sekaran fighter wall. The maneuver resulted in him cutting through several more ships. He tried to keep his ship moving erratically along a vertical plane while firing so he couldn't be targeted as easily by the battleship.

The reinforcements from the *Justicar* met with the Sekaran fighters, and the fight broke loose as if into the Dark Pit itself. Ships swarmed everywhere. The Sekaran wall formation broke, adding to the chaos. Maneuvering without running into another ship proved difficult. It would have been impossible for someone whose reflexes didn't have nanite aide.

As if the thought had tempted fate, Drin's viper's wing collided with one of the Sekaran ships. The accident sent him into a tail-spin. His ship flipped multiple times, and even with the nanites, Drin found himself becoming dizzy. He tried to right himself, but the collision destabilized one of his thrusters. The controls were too difficult to manage while he spun as he did, but he focused and tried anyway.

The AI could compensate for the damaged thruster. He just needed to let it know to do so. Drin ran his finger up the touch screen, pulling up the diagnostics and managed to get the AI working. The ship's rotation slowed, and he finally came to a level resting place.

It took several more moments for Drin to overcome the dizziness. When he did, he saw he had drifted away from the battle, out into open space. He could have been picked off easily if one of the Sekaran ships had targeted him here.

Worse, looking at his tactical screen, it appeared the Sekarans overwhelmed the Elorian forces. There were just too many of them. The battle migrated toward the *Justicar,* away from the Sekaran battleships.

This wasn't good. Drin tried to push his ship forward, but it jolted off to the side. Even though the AI had compensated for the stabilization, the thruster had sustained too much damage. It set Drin even further off course, into the debris field of what used to be Jayden's World.

Rocks smashed against Drin's shields. He worked the controls frantically to try to get himself back into the battle. He couldn't be pushed away from the fight now. His people needed him.

The ship slowed as Drin tried to get the viper back into a mode where it would hover in place. A large piece of rock flew toward him, forcing him to try to evade it. His maneuver didn't take him in the direction he'd hoped. It was frustrating not being able to manage the controls with any efficiency.

His tactical screen blinked red. The Elorians were sustaining heavy casualties.

"I'm hit!" Commander Shayne said through the comm.

Oh, no.

"I'm gonna ram the bastards. Lord forgive my sins. I'm coming home," Shayne said.

The comm went to static.

Drin drifted helplessly, the thrusters failing to react to his commands. He couldn't push his craft in a reliable direction, and he'd be useless back in the battle. All he could do was watch as more waves of Sekaran fighters entered the battlefield. His initial fears of their overwhelming force had come to fruition.

The *Justicar's* crew seemed to notice the change in the battle's dynamic as well, as they repositioned to turn and try to make space between the ship and the Sekarans so they could jump out of the system. "Father Cline to all fighters. Return to mothership. I repeat, return to mothership. We are retreating. You have..." The comm line died in static.

The Sekarans had put up a scattering field, something Drin had seen them do on Deklyn to stop any outgoing transmissions when he had wanted to summon a mercenary fleet to help with the battle there. If only the mercenaries had stuck around and jointed the Elorians, this might have been a fair fight.

There was no point in dwelling on what might have been. He had to figure out what he could do about the situation at hand. Removed from the battle, Drin had his AI system direct repair bots toward his broken thruster. Several small, spider-like bots scurried across the wing and went to work. Based on the AI's diagnostic, it would take an hour to repair. Drin wouldn't be able to get back to the *Justicar* before they jumped.

As he thought about the *Justicar,* the Sekaran fighter swarm descended on the capital ship. The *Justicar's* point defense systems destroyed dozens of them at a time, but the sheer numbers made the destruction of several of their ships not matter. The Sekarans didn't care whether a few of them died. Their warriors were brainwashed by their elders. "Victory or death!" they often cried in their language. None turned back in service of their false prophet, Eltu. They were motivated by promises of riches and concubines in the afterlife.

The thought disgusted Drin, but not more than what he saw on his tactical display. The Sekaran fighters pummeled the

Justicar with their lasers. Almost all of the Elorian fighters had been destroyed. They never had a chance in this battle.

Drin pulled up the ship's camera feed. Wave after wave hit the *Justicar's* shields, and soon, those failed. The laser bolts cut through the hull like a knife would flesh. Metal and sparks shot everywhere. Bodies of his companions were sucked out into space. Everyone he knew, everyone he had ever loved—they weren't going to make it.

How could God allow this to happen? Things had been going so well. They'd liberated worlds, uncovered a terrible Sekaran plot with this superweapon. Couldn't he have mercy on his chosen?

Tears streaked down Drin's face as he watched the carnage. The Sekarans certainly took no mercy on their target. The *Justicar* was obliterated. Father Cline. Sister Vith. They didn't deserve this fate.

Drin slammed his fist against the controls, causing the display screen to crack. The viper made a chirping sound, letting him know of the error in the system. He didn't care. Everything he'd ever fought for, all gone in an instant.

But he was still out here, and the Sekarans would be running search parties soon. He tapped on his broken display, hoping it would still work. He could power down his vessel, rely on his nanites to survive. They might not spot him in the debris field created by the destroyed planet. He could get out of here, warn others what happened.

All the viper's systems turned off, the hum of his engines turning into the heavy silence of space. Drin turned on his communications channel. The Sekarans might drop their scattering field once they thought there were no Elorians present. It was a long shot, but maybe he could intercept some of their communications.

The battle quickly shifted to several of the Elorian fighters jumping out of the system, while the Sekarans shot down every remaining Elorian they could find. They didn't take prisoners. It was utter destruction wherever they went.

Drin turned his cockpit's life support system off, using his nanites to stay alive. His armor suit kept him warm and breathing. He could stay in this condition without outside support for several hours. Eventually, he would need to find some means to eat and replenish his body's natural energy that powered the nanites as surely as any other organ inside of him.

Minutes passed. Drin muttered the Lord's Prayer to himself several times, focusing on God in his moment of peril. Those were the times to turn over to God completely, even if the universe didn't seem fair. His plan would prevail, and Drin had to trust it.

After a time, Sekaran chatter appeared on the comm channels. Drin broke from his reverie and paid attention. It was in their language. He understood some of the words Sekarans said—*battle, victory, Eltu,* but he couldn't make out the specifics. His craft recorded incoming conversations, and his nanites could assist with the translation if he played it back. He willed the nanites into their translation mode, listening to the communication one more time.

On his visor, the translated words appeared:

THE ELORIAN INFIDELS HAVE BEEN DESTROYED. OUR AMBUSH WORKED PERFECTLY, PRAISE ELTU. WE WILL BE RETURNING TO BASE AT ARASU TO ASSIST WITH THE MISSION OF UNCOVERING ANOTHER ANCIENT MACHINE. COPY.

Drin frowned, considering the message. An ancient machine? It sounded strange to him. Had they uncovered some weapon from the past, rather than inventing it? Was this how they were destroying planets like Jayden's World from the inside? He needed more information.

More time passed. The Sekaran fleet finally jumped out of the system. His repairs were nearing their completion. He'd be able to maneuver again and jump himself. The severity of what had happened hit him. It was always a risk, going out and doing battle in the Lord's name. This time, they had lost everything. But he would avenge the deaths of the Lord's saints. If it was the last thing he'd do.

But where would he go? Returning to the fleet without information wouldn't be helpful. He needed to be more useful, and he could poke around the galaxy alone much more easily than with a fleet. It didn't feel right to return to the Elorians and rejoin some new ship, with other Templars he didn't know. No, the Lord directed him to the people who had helped him this past year, the ones he had helped. They would return the favor.

Tapping into his broken control console, he set course to the one place he knew he could regroup and find help to fight the Sekaran menace—Deklyn.

EIGHT

"With a unanimous vote of the council, we usher the planet Deklyn into our Minor Planets Trade Union," Zebee said. A short, bug-like creature with eyes comprised of several different little orbs, which reflected in the soft light of the room, Zebee had antennae, which stood atop his head, fluttering at regular intervals.

Anais let out a breath of relief. Elaym reached over and squeezed her hand. They hadn't been sure if the group would accept them. When trader captain Cohn had invited them into this alliance of worlds, it seemed like a con. But the process was a lot harder than he'd led her to believe.

All she wanted to do was to lie down on a nice guest quarters bed and close her eyes. She'd spent several hours speaking about the trials of her world and listening to the other six species representatives in the room talk about their stories with the Sekarans. From the stories she'd heard, Deklyn got off easy. Most of the others had stories akin to what Err-dio had experienced on Konsin II—brutal slavery, rape of a planet's resources, and sometimes worse.

Her heart broke every time one of them spoke, and she wanted to cry when she heard Err-dio recount the tale of how all of his people were enslaved, forced to brutally work so hard in the hot desert sun to the point where they had to hide and take shifts replacing one another while the tired laborers recovered. If Deklyn had been under Sekaran rule for much longer, it could have been a lot worse than some leveled buildings and a poor trading economy.

"Thank you," Anais said. "I'm happy to join. If you're familiar with Deklyn, we're best known for our exports of strong lumber from our trees, as well as a number of herbs and remedies from our robust ecosystem. We will be helpful for rebuilding worlds or for medicine. We're looking for traders to come in and create shipping routes that were once established to our system."

"We'll ensure that happens," Zebee said. "I hope Arasu may be the first to greet you in commerce and trade. If you'd be willing to forego tariffs on import items, I'm sure my people would do the same."

"You have a deal," Anais said. He'd told her about his world, Arasu. And it sounded like it had a very interesting topography. Rivers carved out long canyons across the world, creating a unique set of waterways for transportation, and natural caves everywhere provided shelter for the residents. They'd survived Sekaran attack by being able to utilize those cave networks and waterways in a manner the invaders couldn't grasp.

It felt good to have accomplished something. A warmth resonated in her, as if it were her rightful place to be making these kinds of pacts between other species. She was tangibly making the universe a better place. Though the nanites buzzed within her, itching for action, they had to remain still for the time being.

"And we'll all meet with you individually to make other agreements," a long-snouted Chinsin woman named Kit said.

"I'd like that," Anais said. "But I'm sure all of us can use a break. It's been a long day discussing tragedy. Should we head back to the bar where we met Cohn? Where is he, anyway?"

"Cohn had other duties to attend to," Zebee said.

"Yes. There was a frightening rumor that an Elorian docked with the station. I'm not sure why Parthenon would allow them here, but Cohn was going to confirm it."

Err-dio rushed to his feet. "Do you think..."

Anais stood much more slowly. "It could be anyone. We can't just assume it's him." She turned back to Zebee who appeared as confused as his bug face could express. "Do you happen to know where Cohn went? Can we meet up with him?"

"I don't see why not," Zebee said. He slid a bar on his wrist comm and called up the tall trader captain. "Cohn, do you read?"

"I do. I'm a little busy right now. Can I call you back?"

"Our new members want to meet you. They seem very excited to see the Elorian."

Cohn laughed through the comm. "Who could be excited to see one of them? Where they go, so goes death."

Anais wanted to protest, but to outsiders, it often seemed like the Sekarans and Elorians fought one another with no concern for who they harmed in the process. Without intimate knowledge of the realities of the battles, one might think the two species and their religions were much the same.

Anais, however, learned very quickly that there were stark differences between the two, most notably the Elorian concern for life. This wasn't the time to debate her newfound friends, however. She needed them to work with their worlds to uplift Deklyn, and she couldn't let her personal biases get in the way of the mission.

Zebee looked to Anais as if to confirm. Anais nodded. "They're insistent," Zebee said.

Cohn sighed. "Tell them to meet me at the level five conference centers. Apparently, the Elorian has been storming around here looking for someone. He's making all kinds of people nervous."

Anais leaned over Zebee's wrist so she could speak into the

comm. "We'll be right there! Wait for us." She started toward the door but looked back. "Do you think someone could lead us to the conference area?"

Zebee motioned to one of his subordinates, who moved to the door. Err-dio followed dutifully behind Anais, but Elaym remained seated. "I'll stay here if you don't mind. I'd like to work out some more of the details of our trade negotiations."

"Good idea," Anais said. Should she leave Elaym alone to make the deals without her? Part of her itched inside as if she were reneging in her duties, but Drin might be here! How could she focus on anything else with the prospect of seeing him looming over her? She would have to trust Elaym.

They said their goodbyes, and she departed with Zebee's aide.

The trip to the fifth level didn't take too long. A lift was positioned close to the room they'd been occupying for their meetings. When they reached the area, it was fairly quiet. Several business attire-clad aliens in dark colors walked the corridors. They seemed in a hurry to get out of the hall they'd come from—the same direction Anais was heading. They caught up to Cohn.

"I don't understand what you could possibly want with an Elorian," Cohn said, not bothering to greet them.

"What do you want with him?" Anais asked.

"Intel."

They proceeded forward in silence until the paths branched into three very long corridors. Each was dimly lit with a slightly different color to mark which section's conference rooms they were, but the halls all looked the same otherwise.

"Which way?" Anais asked.

Before Cohn could answer, Anais turned to the left and saw the distinct green features of an Elorian. Tall, with a short, buzzed haircut. Even from behind, Anais recognized him. Her heart raced in anticipation, and she sped down the hallway at as fast a pace as her heart beat. "Drin!" she called.

NINE

The girl pummeled into Drin. If she had been a hair slower, he might have formed his nanite shield and light sword and cut her into pieces. She had come on like an attack, and the way she squeezed him so tightly, it almost seemed like she *was* trying to kill him. Drin chuckled all the same, happy to have found her at last. He threw his arms around her and returned the embrace.

"I missed you," Anais said.

"I wasn't gone all that long," Drin said.

She pulled back and looked up at him, big eyes shining at him. Was it a look of adoration? She cared for him too much...and he cared for her too much, as well. "Still," Anais said. "What are you doing here?"

Three others rushed down the hallway, two from races Drin didn't recognize, and the other, a Skree—Err-dio.

"Templar Drin! The Lord blesses us with your presence."

"Don't tell me you're a part of their cult," the tallest of the group said. He scoffed.

Anais turned. "Cohn, it's a religion, not a cult. And there's merit to it."

Cohn shook his head, looking like he was about ready to take off running. It was a fight-or-flight instinct. Drin had seen it in a number species during his time as a Templar. Either way, this man hated his people. Drin could feel it resonating from him.

"I'm not going to get roped into this," Cohn said.

"Perhaps it's best we speak alone," Drin said to Anais.

Anais looked back at the others. "Would you mind waiting for us?"

Err-dio held his expression flat, but Drin could tell he wanted in on the conversation as well, and so he motioned Err-dio over with him and Anais. The other two lingered in the hallway, looks of both rage and confusion on their faces.

Anais pressed her hand against one of the conference rooms' door scanners. It opened, revealing a vacant room inside. "I have an account here now. We can utilize station amenities."

"Much better than last time we came here," Err-dio said. They all went inside, and the door closed behind them.

"I'm still confused as to why you're here," Anais said.

"I came looking for you," Drin said.

"But I didn't tell you I was coming to Parthenon Station."

"No. I went to Deklyn first, sent a signal down to the planet, and Lyssa answered to tell me where you'd gone." Drin turned to Err-dio. "Thank you for keeping her safe."

Anais crossed her arms, frowning as if insulted. "I can do fine on my own, thank you very much."

Both men looked at her incredulously, and the three of them burst out laughing together. "It does feel like we've spent a longer time apart than we have," Drin said. "Much has changed since we last spoke."

"Oh?" Anais asked.

"The *Justicar* is no more," Drin said.

Err-dio gasped. "No. I can't believe it."

"It's so."

The room fell into silence. Anais and Err-dio seemed to be more in shock about the news than Drin had been when he'd witnessed the battle firsthand. People died in war. Drin had lost many friends, many brothers. This wasn't the first time, and he was sure it wouldn't be the last.

Though these two had experienced a few battles, they didn't understand the life of a warrior. They had the impression that Templars were somehow invincible. Though his people had abilities beyond most in battle, it still didn't free them from the dangerous realities of war each time they fought.

"I'm sorry, Drin," Anais said in a near whisper.

"I've prayed over my brothers, and I have to do honor by their sacrifices. It's part of why I want to speak with you."

"What happened?" Err-dio asked.

Drin dove into the story, telling them of the intelligence about a Sekaran superweapon, how the weapon was already functional and deployed on Jayden's World, and how the planet burst before his very eyes. He detailed the ambush, and how he'd survived because of a thruster malfunction that made him drift away from the main battle, unable to do anything.

"The Lord willed you apart from the slaughter for a purpose," Err-dio said.

Drin hadn't considered that his survival had been part of God's plan. Of course it was. Everything had a purpose. But he'd been too caught up in the moments, in the battles, and in the deaths of his companions to be able to reflect on the personal matters of the situation.

His life had gone much this way ever since he'd abandoned his ship the first time on Konsin II. Drin tried to run, tried to go different ways, but the Lord always brought him to this path. Whatever this path was. He couldn't be certain, he just prayed he could follow what the Lord wanted, and that he wouldn't be clouded by his own selfish judgment.

"Good point," Drin said finally.

He resumed his story of the battle, up until he intercepted the message. "And the Sekarans said they had a base on a world called Arasu."

Anais' eyes went wide.

"What?" Drin asked.

"We just met representatives from Arasu. You know the bug creature outside?" She made a mean expression and stuck two fingers up over her head, which Drin assumed meant to signify the creature's antennae.

"I saw the creature."

"He's from Arasu." Anais turned to Err-dio. "We just made a trade deal with them. They said their world had been overrun, but they survived it. How could the Sekarans have a base there?"

"They could be lying to you," Drin said.

Anais bit her lip. "I don't think so. They seem pretty honest to me. But I don't know. I could try to investigate a little?"

"The last time you tried to investigate what was happening with your friend on Altequine, I had to come and rescue you," Drin said. It seemed so long ago. She stared at him with big eyes, but not as innocent as they had been before. She could handle herself better now. Drin could see it in her. She'd better, because he'd trained her to fight.

"You know it'll be different this time." In a sudden move, Anais pressed her hand to Drin's chest.

Err-dio whistled and slipped away from them. "I am sure there's something elsewhere to do. Important," he said, his words hurried.

Drin flinched, but he didn't recoil from Anais' action, nor could he bring himself to respond to Err-dio's words. It was just so sudden. The touch. The warmth of her hand. It was as if it pierced through is nanite-created clothing. His heart pounded a little harder, and he hoped she wouldn't notice it. "I do."

"Then trust me?" Anais ticked the corner of her lips up into a small smile.

"I don't want you to get hurt."

"I know."

They fell silent, her still touching him. Their eyes locked, but what could they do? This wasn't right. He couldn't do this. He'd already resigned himself to being celibate, and if the tension in the air became any thicker, he'd tear her apart. God, how he wanted to...

No. Drin shut his eyes tightly.

"It's okay, Drin," Anais said. "I won't make you violate your vows."

"You know what I'm thinking," Drin said. "Ever since our nanite fields merged."

"It wouldn't take any sensory enhancements to tell what you're thinking now," Anais said. She lowered her hand. Drin missed the touch but kept his eyes closed. Even in his self-inflicted darkness, he could see her in his mind's eye. This was terrible.

"What do I do?"

"Do what you have to do," Anais said.

Drin clenched his jaw tighter. He wanted the feelings to go away—and they wouldn't. "I love you, Anais." He opened his eyes again.

She stood where he had left her, staring up at him, her long ears flopped to one side. Even though she'd been through the horrors of war, the tyranny of slavery, she remained an innocent. Her brightness was infectious, and he longed to be around her.

It was a tremendous relief to get the words off his chest. *I love you.* He hadn't thought of how much those words rang true before. He had admitted he cared for Anais, but not to this extent. It still left him with tremendous conflict inside. His Templar order renounced all attachments, which meant relationships just like this were forbidden. The closest thing he'd ever had to an attachment was with his brothers in his unit, and that was a very different feeling.

He didn't know what to do about Anais. It drove him crazy. He wanted to be near her all of the time, wanted to protect her, but he shouldn't.

"You're not saying anything," he said to her.

"I'm trying to let you sort out your own feelings," Anais said. "I know it has to be hard for you."

"How do you deal with it?" Drin asked.

Anais shrugged. "I was never *taught* my feelings are bad."

"But you have them for me?" Drin meant the words to come out as a definitive statement, but he found himself questioning. It mattered to him, and it made him nervous. Why should it make him nervous?

"Of course I do. You know this. Open yourself to the nanites like I have."

Open himself to the nanites? Drin wanted to laugh. He had spent so much time trying to train her in the nanite abilities that he'd taken for granted his own capabilities, but there might be something to having a fresh perspective on the tiny devices. Yezuah had brought her to him for a reason, and perhaps this was part of it.

He took in a deep breath, felt the nanites buzzing through and around him. The tiny machines orbited both him and her, and they intertwined together. They communicated, they touched, shared energies. Drin stifled a breath as he focused in on the nanites' reactions. He had no idea they were interacting at this intense of a level. It was electrifying.

And then he felt it. It didn't come from inside him—those feelings came from inside *her*. Warmth. Love. Affection. She cared about him as intensely as he did her—perhaps more.

It was all too much. Drin had come here to try to solve problems of a galactic scale, but these very personal, intimate problems scared him much more than a Sekaran superweapon. It was irrational. He didn't like it. "This is contrary to my vows."

"Is it? We haven't done anything physical. I can't believe, given what I've read in your scriptures, that Yezuah would be opposed to love."

"You're getting dangerously close to heresy," Drin said.

"You're thinking too much," Anais said. "I'm here with you. Enjoy it. Live in the moment. The nanites have these abilities because Yezuah wanted his people to be connected, to act as his body. Not alone, but together."

It was the kind of thing he'd tell any new recruit learning to use their nanites. One had to stop thinking so much and just go with the flow of the electrical fields the nanites created. It was hard to do for someone first attempting to control the tiny machines, but Drin could do it easily now. Why was this so different? Anais was right.

He tried to calm his mind, to do his breathing exercises. He'd done them many times before, settled himself in meditation and in prayer, but this time was different. It was so hard to shut down his mind.

Anais cocked her head curiously at him. "You're really unsettled. I'm sorry, I didn't mean to—"

"It's okay," Drin said. "But we should focus on the task at hand. I was worried about your safety, but I do agree that you've grown in your abilities and the way you conduct yourself. I know you can handle yourself."

"Thank you." Anais clasped her hands together. "First thing's first. I should rejoin my friends and see how Elaym's doing with negotiations down below. I can dig a little into this Arasu planet and gather some information for you. They've been friendly so far, so I'm sure they'll provide it. You can look it over, then we can figure out a plan. Deal?"

Drin nodded. "You're getting better with patience and understanding the necessity of preparation before action."

Anais winked. "I'll take the compliment. She spun on her heel, her tail twitching behind her as she exited the conference room door.

TEN

Cohn did not look pleased to see her.

When she had left the trader captain and Zebee's assistant, they had been skeptical about her speaking with Drin. Now, they looked at her in a downright cold manner. "Let's head back to check on Zebee and Elaym, shall we?" Anais asked, trying to keep her tone upbeat.

"Why didn't you tell us you worked with Elorians?" Cohn asked. He crossed his lanky arms over one another.

"I didn't think about it. I don't work with him, either. He's my friend," Anais said.

"Elorians don't make friends, they make converts," Cohn said.

Zebee's assistant looked very confused, the bug-like creature seeming not to want to get in the middle of the conversation. Anais didn't blame him. She didn't much want to confront Cohn, either. "You're wrong. They're people like anyone else. Why does everyone have to be so quick to judge an entire species?"

"Because of the destruction they bring. We should remove him from the station, or see if security will do it for us," Cohn said.

"You'll do nothing of the sort. Now, can I please get back to my people? We have much more important things to do than to try to hurt Drin."

Cohn gritted his teeth and turned. Zebee's assistant moved with him, and soon, the three of them had traveled down the lift and back to the meeting room where the representatives from various worlds had gathered.

Elaym was still hashing out details, leaning over a desk that held a data pad. Zebee hunched over with him, both pointing to different items on the screen and making comments. Anais was glad she missed the details of boring trade negotiations. If things had been different, she might be in a position where she was working for her father doing those very same tasks now. Even though she missed him, it was a minor blessing that she had other options in life.

"What's going on?" Anais asked.

The two men looked up. Elaym smiled. "Working out the first agreement with the Arasu. It looks like they're very interested in the sap from our Greenwood trees. In exchange, they're willing to send us metal alloys for construction. It's simple, but best to start that way to see if this will work. We're going to have no tariffs either way, and hopefully, be able to keep our merchant vessels on standard trade lanes between our worlds from here on out."

Zebee tapped the end of one of his stalky arms onto the datapad. "That should finalize it on our end. Thank you for making this easy."

"No, thank *you*," Elaym said. The two stood.

"I think it's time for me to retire, and I'll need to contact my homeworld," Zebee said.

"We should probably do the same," Anais said. She tried to catch Elaym's eyes. "Drin's here."

"Oh?" Elaym asked."

"Yes. I think we should all chat together."

"Sounds good by me," Elaym said. He collected his datapad.

The rest of the assembled species had all broken into smaller parties similarly. Most appeared to be wrapping up their negotiations just like Elaym and Zebee had done. Anais scanned the room in case someone wanted to speak with them, but seeing no one was paying much attention to her, she slipped out the door with her friends.

The whole Deklyn entourage joined her in the corridors, along with Err-dio. She was excited to reunite with Drin, even if he brought her disconcerting news. She could hardly believe the Templars lost their entire ship. Anais had so many memories with them. Even though she hadn't spent all that long on the *Justicar*, it felt like a second home to her in many ways.

She would miss the nun, Vith, the most. The woman had taken a lot of time and care with Anais, and she was one of the first who believed in her, making Anais feel welcome and useful. It had done wonders for her confidence, she realized. Anais's heart sank, thinking about the woman being gone.

Anais turned to Err-dio. "You want to fetch Drin? Let's meet back at the transient bar. I could really use something to eat."

Err-dio nodded. "I remember where he is. I'll grab him."

"Good," Anais said. She motioned to the rest of the delegation to follow her, and the party moved to the same place they'd been frequenting. Once Anais found a place she liked to dine, she tended to fall into the habit of returning.

It was much more packed today than it had been before. Listening to some conversations, she learned a large starliner cruise had made its stop at the station, creating an influx of tourists. It didn't matter to Anais, she could wait. Things had been going very well for her and her people, even if the Elorians weren't having the same kind of luck. She wished the universe could work in a way where everyone could have good times and peace, but she understood as long as the Sekarans were out there conquering and pillaging worlds, it would be unlikely to happen.

The thought soured her mood, and it must have shown, because Elaym looked at her, concerned. "Why aren't you happy? We're doing what we set out to."

"Something Drin told me."

Elaym's ears perked. "Are you and he—"

"No," Anais said hastily. "I mean, yes. I don't know. It's a complicated thing."

"Huh," Elaym said.

"Don't worry about it. It's not a personal matter that's upsetting me. Drin lost his ship. They were ambushed by Sekarans, and all of his friends are gone."

"Oh." Elaym frowned. "I'm sorry to hear that."

The AI host approached to let them know their table was ready, and they passed several full tables of galactic travelers before stopping at the same table they'd been at the day prior. The familiar felt good on this foreign station. Anais took her seat, as did the others. "Yeah," Anais said to Elaym, resuming her conversation. "They have a weapon that can destroy worlds from the inside. It's frightening."

"It sounds it. Do you think they'll use it on Deklyn?"

"I don't know. But we have to stop them."

Their party ordered their drinks and food. Elaym splurged on some extra appetizers, which seemed to make his people happy. Anais recognized her own need to eat, but thinking of the Elorians, she felt more sick than hungry. When the food came, she gingerly picked at the finger food but didn't order much of her own. It would have to sustain her for now.

Waiting for Drin and Err-dio took longer than she'd hoped. Everyone's moods were so jovial, as they should be. The Deklyn finally made progress in restoring trade to their world. Even though she'd told Elaym, she didn't want to dampen the moods of the others. This was a victory. They deserved to relish in it, even if frightening matters loomed over the horizon. And these were traders and house servants with Elaym and her. They couldn't help her with what was to come, even if she wanted them to.

It would be up to her, Drin, and Err-dio, but she dreaded the moment she would have to act. She'd hoped her days of fighting were over.

She found the environment of all the people in the bar to be stifling. It'd be impossible to get fresh air on a station like this, but she could at least get away from the crowd. Anais slid out of her chair. "I'm going to go find a 'fresher."

"Want us to order you anything?" Elaym asked.

Anais shook her head. "Not right now. I'll figure it out when I get back. You go ahead."

Elaym nodded and returned to the conversation with the others.

No one in the restaurant took any particular note of Anais when she made her way out of it. She passed the refresher room, hoping none at her table would notice. Her goal was just to go somewhere quiet, peaceful. Hopefully, by the time she calmed down and sorted herself out, Drin and Err-dio would be back.

It was odd, this feeling of anxiety. Her chest constricted, making it difficult to breathe. It was all in her head, of course. Her nanites would warn her of any pending health issues if there were something serious. She hadn't used them much since she arrived on the station. When she walked, she pulled up a visor display, allowing her access to her vital signs, a view of infrared spectrums, and a standard power display. The nanites were at one hundred percent, which made sense given their lack of use.

She continued into a corridor, weaving her way around the station. What she'd love at the moment would be to see the stars. But where was there a viewport on the station?

A station worker came by, and Anais asked the question. The

kind gentleman pointed her in the direction of an observation lounge, and Anais happily started off.

Voices spoke around a corner. Anais stopped in her tracks. She recognized one of the voices even from her distance, whispery and gravely—Zebee. The other voice was clearly Cohn. Her Deklyn hearing gave her an advantage, allowing her to listen in without proceeding further, even though the voices spoke in a low tone. After their negotiations, she probably shouldn't eavesdrop on them, but Anais couldn't help but be curious.

"Excellent work today," Zebee said.

"Except the Elorian. Did you know these people were tied in with them?" Cohn asked.

"No. It's a surprise to me, as well. I'm going to have a conversation with Warlord Giot and see what our instructions will be."

Anais froze. Warlord? The Sekarans used such terminology, but they weren't the only ones in the galaxy to use the word. Perhaps she was just paranoid.

"I don't know. He's not going to be happy about this. One of his sworn enemies on the station? And he's working with people we're bringing in? It's going to lead to trouble," Cohn said.

No, paranoia wasn't the problem. It was these people she'd aligned with. She'd had a feeling it had all been too easy. Elaym was going to be devastated. Why would ambassadors from these worlds pretend to be savaged by the Sekarans only to be working for them? The deception made her blood boil. She wanted to form a light sword and scare the pants off these men.

But it wouldn't do any good if she did. She'd been too rash to act in the past, and she wouldn't make a mistake like that now. What would Drin do? He would calm himself and follow them. She nodded to herself, resolving to do just that.

"We can't leave him in the dark just because he might be angry. Come on, let's go find him," Zebee said.

Anais listened to their footsteps falling further from her,

waiting for a safe distance. She willed her nanites to change her clothes to dark robes, ones that would conceal her ears. If they did happen to look back, perhaps they wouldn't spot her. She had to be careful and keep her distance. After one glance around her to make sure no one spotted her, Anais turned the corner and padded after them.

ELEVEN

Drin took his time to meditate on the situation after Anais left. She was working with people from Arasu, and he had hard information that the Sekarans had made a base there. It wasn't going to end well if Anais worked too closely with the Arasu, but she had to follow the path she had set out for the good of her world.

Personal elements to this situation clouded his judgment. He loved her. She loved him. Attachment. Everything the Templars had professed against, and he'd let his emotions get the best of him. It was much easier to think about when she wasn't present. Perhaps chemical pheromones interfered with his rational thought when she stood in front of him. No, it was an excuse.

Regardless, he couldn't pursue the train of thought further. He had a mission to accomplish.

Anais wasn't likely to find out real tactical information from some trade delegation. It was possible the Sekarans operated on Arasu in secret. The representatives here might not even know anything about the Sekarans.

Drin had some tough decisions to make. Anais didn't need to

get caught up in his battles. She needed protection from them, if anything.

Before he could come up with a solution, Err-dio came bounding down the corridor.

"Templar Drin," he said. "Anais sent me to find you."

"Oh?"

"Yes, we're dining and drinking at a transient bar in celebration of the trade negotiations we've completed with Arasu."

"Hmm."

Err-dio cocked his head. "You don't seem pleased. Is it because of what you stated? The Sekarans making their way to the planet?"

"Yes."

"Perhaps you misheard?"

"I'm sure I didn't." Drin shook his head.

"The people in the room all had stories about how their worlds were ransacked by Sekarans. They didn't seem to be the types who would be interested in working with them," Err-dio said.

"Perhaps they're being coerced. Or perhaps the people in the room don't know," Drin said.

"So what do you want to do, then?"

"I'm not sure," Drin said. He folded his hands together, considering. The best way to keep Anais out of danger would be to keep her out of this completely. "I think we don't return to Anais."

"Are you sure?" Err-dio said. "I think she would want to know what we're doing."

"She would. But to keep her safe, it's better to keep her out of our plans. Besides, we may not find anything. We wouldn't want to alarm her if these people she met are innocents."

"I don't like it," Err-dio said.

"I don't either," Drin said. "But I believe it's the right course. You should come with me, and we can depart for Arasu together."

Err-dio frowned. "You are stubborn, Templar Drin, but I will follow your command."

Drin nodded, making his way for the shuttle bay before Err-dio could find a reason to convince him to stay. It would be better for Anais this way. She had her path, and he had his. At least, he tried to convince himself of such.

It still grated on him despite his decision to protect her by keeping her away from the conflict. Err-dio was right, she wouldn't like it. But he couldn't make his decisions in the matter of this Holy War based on whether a woman would appreciate his move.

They reached the shuttle bay in silence, Err-dio joining Drin in his viper in the co-piloting location. It was cramped behind Drin, rarely used by Templars except in emergencies. "I'm sorry about the accommodations."

"I will use the time to deny the flesh and reflect upon the sins I have committed," Err-dio.

Drin strapped himself in and chuckled. "Careful. The Lord knows your heart, and if your contrition is insincere..."

"Trust me, I'm already receiving my penance back here."

The cockpit closed. Drin waited until he was given the signal to depart by the shuttle bay control officer, and he set course for Arasu. As they left Parthenon Station, Drin looked back over his shoulder, unable to help but feel guilt for leaving Anais without saying a word. She would understand. At least, he hoped she would.

TWELVE

As Zebee and Cohn meandered through the station, Anais gained confidence in her ability to sneak around. At first, she had been worried. If they spotted her, even in her current attire, it could wreck everything. But as they moved on, they didn't so much as spare a glance back in her direction.

Most of her targets' conversations had been personal as they crossed through the station. Cohn asked about Zebee's latest egg clutch, apparently well over a thousand strong. It was amazing to think of so many young beings coming into existence so quickly. Anais wondered how they didn't overpopulate the entire galaxy.

Cohn didn't have any children, she learned. He and his brothers each went their separate ways upon private trading vessels.

When they reached the open market area of Parthenon Station, Anais lost track of their conversation amongst the background noise of the crowd. She weaved in between people, trying not to lose sight of her targets ahead of her. This was a critical moment in her plan to follow them to their warlord. If she lost them amongst the shoppers and merchants, she wouldn't be able to find out what they were planning.

For a brief moment, she considered turning back. They were meeting with Sekarans, which was frightening enough. Even though she had held back from confronting them, this still was a hasty move on her part. She should be consulting with Drin, talking to him.

Thinking of Drin caused her to lose focus. Did she want to be with him to give him a report on the subject or because she wanted to be with him? It was impossible to tell. His confession of his love for her had been so sudden, and she'd hardly had any time to think about it. She'd hoped she would have more time to reflect on the electrifying moment between them, but here she was.

The table! Her friends would still be back eating, wondering where she went. Oh, well. They were the least of her problems if they'd inadvertently agreed to be a part of a trade relationship with Sekarans. She found herself angry with Cohn and Zebee. How dare they conceal their true motives from her?

There could still be another explanation. She didn't know the reason they were meeting with this Sekaran. Just that he existed. Her heart raced. Any moment now, she'd be able to see for certain. Of course, they probably would have a meeting behind closed doors. She would have to rely on her Deklyn hearing, aided by the nanites, to get good information.

The men moved into a different corridor. Anais was grateful that they hadn't headed to one of the lifts. If they'd changed levels, there would have been no telling if she could find them again on a station this size. She kept her distance like she had before, tiptoeing through the corridor to try not to make a sound and alert them.

The sound of footsteps around the corner came to a stop. Anais held herself back.

One of her targets rang the door chime to a room, which echoed in a muffled fashion into the corridor. Air piping through the ventilation systems rumbled in the corridor. The door *whooshed* open.

"You have good news?" a gruff voice asked. Right to the point, angry almost.

"Some good, and some bad. Can we come in?" Cohn asked. "We shouldn't talk about this in the hallway."

"If you insist," the gruff voice said. The door shut.

The men went inside, leaving her in the corridor alone. Anais peeked around the corner and, seeing it was clear, moved forward. This was her moment. She would listen and find out what she could as quickly as possible, lest anyone see her eavesdropping. She made her way to the door and pressed her ear against the crack where it closed. She could barely make out conversation.

"Very good. A governor lost this world because of his ineptitude. I'm trying to convince the rest of the council we should pursue a way of conquest through trade. Once we have established a strong arm economically, we can make worlds bend to our wills much more easily, and with much less resentment in the population."

Anais' eyes widened. She'd been brought before a warlord, planning his conquest of non-Sekaran systems, and he told her his plan. Create this coalition of worlds where they could talk about their mutual hatred of the Sekarans, and yet pull the strings economically. In long term, it could work really well. If the Sekarans gained control of economies, they could influence governments, change the course of civilizations over generations. It was a patient strategy, not one she'd seen from the other Sekarans. This course of action frightened her much more than normal Sekaran attacks. It was insidious.

"You can spare us the lecture," Cohn said. "We're on board as long as the credits keep flowing."

"Eventually, you too will see the grace of Eltu and renounce your secular ways," the gruff voice said.

"Doubt it," Cohn huffed.

"Let's not get off track," Zebee said. "You said you would free the slaves in the ever-flowing fields if we brought you trade contracts. We have done so."

"And the slaves will be freed. As soon as the contracts are completely executed. Paper is worthless. Action is everything," said the warlord.

"That wasn't the agreement."

"Do you imply I'm a liar?" the warlord challenged.

"No, no I wouldn't," Zebee said.

"There is one other matter," Cohn said.

"Yes?"

"There's an Elorian on the station. And he's befriended one of our Deklyn representatives," Cohn said.

"What?" The warlord sounded incensed. "He must have been one of the Elorians who liberated their world from our idiot governor. I was assured all of them were summarily wiped out of this galaxy, however. This is disconcerting."

"What do we do about it?" Cohn asked.

"Find the Elorian and kill him," the warlord said with a matter-of-factness that made Anais shiver.

All of her worst fears were confirmed. She had to find Drin and warn him before they could do something. It had been a mistake to throw in with this group. She wished she'd been able to see it earlier.

Anais spun to try to run back down the corridor, and she nearly collided with someone. "I'm sorry," she said, as she dodged to the side. When she looked up, she saw a man with Sekaran features. He grinned at her.

"Yes, you will be." He had a laser-repeater in his hand, and he shot her, point-blank.

Anais tried to get her nanite shield up, but she was too late. The pain overwhelmed her, causing her to scream. Her eyes rolled back, losing focus on the world. She could feel her body going limp, and everything went dark.

THIRTEEN

Drin approached Arasu. The world didn't seem to have much in terms of planetary defenses. Similar to Deklyn, which had a few satellites that couldn't track them the first time they approached Anais's world.

Unlike Deklyn, however, this planet wasn't filled with lush life. It had waterways that weaved through spots of dark brown dirt and rock-like veins. A patch in the north appeared to have dried up, withered—a shell of its former glory. The area was large enough to spot from space.

No defenses seemed to trigger as he and Err-dio approached the planet. Nor was there contact. Shifting his scanners to search for biological life, he found that the bulk of the population appeared to be underground.

"I'm not sure where we should set down," Drin said.

Err-dio tapped frantically into his controls behind Drin. The Skree's thick fingers pressed hard against the screen in little thuds. "I'm spotting a massive energy build up. Relaying the coordinates to your display console."

The coordinates appeared on the display—forty-five degrees longitude north of the equator by twenty-three degrees latitude from the planet's median. In the dead zone. Drin set the autopilot to take them to that location. They descended into the atmosphere.

"How were you able to spot the signature?" Drin asked.

"I reprogrammed your sensors to search for it. I figured if there's a superweapon, it would have to be something that creates a lot of energy," Err-dio said.

"You know how to reprogram ship sensors?"

"I worked on sky-bikes in Altequine, repairing them for the Sekarans. A lot of the time, I had to take components for my people so we could send messages. We worked with what we had. Your systems are much easier to operate than a piecemeal comm system, let me tell you." Err-dio chuckled.

Drin had forgotten Err-dio was so competent with devices. They'd been through so much over the past few months, Altequine seemed like a lifetime ago. Err-dio had always shown an aptitude in such matters. He should have had the Templars put him to more effective work in an engineering capacity. But, if he had, the Skree wouldn't be here with him now, aiding him in this vastly important mission. God's plan unfolded in the strangest of ways.

The autopilot landing protocols took them into a crevice, with two steep walls on either side. The viper descended in a straight line, using its bottom thrusters to ease them into a landing position. Large rock faces stretched upward on either side of them, reds and browns in different layers.

"The atmosphere appears breathable," Err-dio said.

"Good," Drin said. The thrusters turned off as they touched down, and he popped the cockpit so he could get out.

Err-dio stood quickly, stretching his back and arms. "I thought I'd never get out of there."

"There's a reason we tend to fly with one pilot," Drin said. "The extra seat is useful, though, for when the necessity arises."

"Indeed," Err-dio said.

Drin formed his armor around him, not about to let himself get ambushed on a Sekaran-controlled world. His nanites immediately detected the energy source his craft had shown and found a cave opening about a quarter-mile ahead. "This way," Drin said, jumping down from the craft.

Err-dio descended the small ladder and followed Drin through the former river bed.

They plodded their way through the soft dirt and rocks. Though Drin had his armor on, he saw the temperature was cool outside. Winds blew heavily above, but they seemed to be sheltered from it in the dried river bed where they stood. Drin turned to ensure Err-dio was keeping up with him. The Skree's breaths were labored. "Are you okay?"

"Yes, Templar Drin. The air is thin on this world is all."

"We'll be there soon," Drin said.

They reached the entrance to the cave, which was no more than a small crack in the wall of the easternmost rock face. The AI wouldn't steer them wrong, but as it was, they wouldn't be able to get inside.

"Stand back," Drin said. He formed a light sword in his hand.

Err-dio took several steps backward.

Drin drove his light sword into the rock, bringing the energy blade up and down, blasting the wall into bits. Dust flew everywhere, as did rocks, as they cracked off the wall. He kept at it for a long time, until his blade met no resistance. Then he waited for the dust to settle.

An opening had formed where there once was but a small crack. It was dark inside, no light inside from anywhere near their location. The energy source was ahead and below. Drin hoped this opening would lead them into a proper shaft.

He stepped inside, his night vision kicking into view on his visor.

Err-dio grabbed him by the arm. "I can't see."

"I will be your eyes. Walk with me, and stay close," Drin said. He held his palm up, creating a ball of light with the nanites to give them a little glow by which to see, but he didn't dare make it too bright, lest they run into enemies ahead. They had to proceed with caution on this strange world.

He moved forward into the darkness, much more carefully than he would have alone. Err-dio managed to follow. They eventually came to a passage where there were some soft goo-lights hanging in the corridor. This place was inhabited.

"I think we're on the right track," Err-dio said.

Drin nodded. He scanned the area as it bisected. The energy signature seemed to still be below them, but more to the right. He opted to take that path.

The cave structure changed. All around him were large, hexagonal insets, with what looked like melted wax dripping from them. He could have reached his hand inside, but he didn't dare, not sure what he would find there.

Err-dio touched one of the hexagons. It snapped off easily. "These are strange walls."

"Yes. Whatever this is, it isn't natural," Drin said.

They continued through the strange corridor. It sloped downward as Drin had hoped and opened up into a giant cavern with stalactites hanging from the ceiling. A gooey liquid dripped from some of them.

Drin found himself at the edge of a cliff. He stared downward into a giant chasm. It took a moment for his visor to adjust to the view. Figures stood below, bipedal, but it was impossible to make them out in this level of light and distance. The bipedals surrounded a large, metallic device with rings that circled around it. This was the object that created the energy signature, drawing Drin here.

"I can't see a thing," Err-dio said. He tried to whisper, but his voice still carried and echoed through the chasm.

Drin pushed Err-dio back. He shouldn't have said a word. The figures below stirred and looked up toward them.

Laser bolts buzzed in their direction. Some hit stalactites above, severing the connection of the rocks to the cave and causing deadly, sharp objects to fall from overhead.

"Run," Drin said, pushing Err-dio back the direction they'd come. The Skree did as Drin asked, careful about his footing. The laser fire continued, some bumping into Drin's nanite shielding. None got through too much.

They returned to the corridor of the strange hexagons, out of range of the lasers below.

"I'd say we found the right spot," Err-dio said.

"Yes, but they know we're here," Drin said. This wasn't good. They didn't have an element of surprise, and there were just two of them against an army.

They found their way back to where the corridor split into two. Could they find allies on this world? Arasu had a species who inhabited it, not Sekarans. Surely, they couldn't all be loyal to their captors.

The smart decision would be to go back to the ship, to reunite with the Templars, and bring others here to help. Would there be time for the intelligent choice? The device below appeared to be functional. The rings spun on it, and it generated an immense amount of energy. If this was the Sekarans' world destroyer, there might not be time for a trip off-planet to find more of his people and convince them to come here.

The dilemma ate at Drin, causing his throat to constrict. Nervousness overcame him like it hadn't in a long time. He had to make the right decision, or billions of lives could be at risk.

As they pushed toward the exit, Drin became lost in thought. The sound of laser-repeaters powering up ahead pulled him back to reality.

A unit of Sekaran soldiers stood in front of him, their weapons pointed at his chest.

FOURTEEN

When Anais awoke, she expected to find herself on the floor of some dark cell, but instead, she appeared to be in a small cabin on a bed. No one had touched her, she still had her nanite-formed robes covering her body. It meant whoever had captured her didn't know she had the Elorian nanites, which at least was one positive thing.

Her head hurt. She had been hit by a laser-repeater. It should have blown a hole in her. She reached down to her stomach, where the blasts had hit. It didn't hurt. Had the nanites protected her even though she didn't have time to form a normal shield before she was ambushed?

The door to her quarters opened. Anais sat up quickly. Her instincts kicked in for her to protect herself, causing her to tense her body. Two soldiers stood at the door, laser-repeaters pointed at her. She'd expected the guards to be Sekarans, but they were the Arasu—Zebee's people.

"Where am I?" Anais asked.

"The transport ship Odez. Now come with us," one of the guards said.

She'd been moved to a transport ship. Which meant she was out in the middle of space. Escape would be difficult. If she were Drin, she'd activate her nanites and tear through this ship, commandeer it, and make her way to Deklyn to get reinforcements. But she wasn't Drin. Her fighting abilities could only be considered questionable at best, even with the aid of the nanites. Her mind wandered to the moment back on Deklyn where she'd been overwhelmed by Sekaran soldiers. They'd nearly killed her. It'd taken Drin to bring her back from the brink.

For now, she had to assess the situation and comply with their demands.

"Where?" Anais asked, standing. She moved slowly, keeping her hands up, just in case they were trigger happy.

"Warlord Redell wishes to dine with you this evening."

It was already evening time. At least they gave her some information. "Dine?" All of it confused her nonetheless.

"Yes. You are to be his guest. If you would come this way?" The guard motioned to the corridor.

Anais made her way toward them. The guards gave her room to exit the door and head into the corridor, before leading her around the ship. The hallways were much tighter than in the station, and the walls had odd, hexagonal patterns to them. They shined and glinted as she passed each one, her reflection distorting in the golden metal of their shapes.

They led her up a couple of levels and toward what she presumed to be the fore of the ship. Large double doors opened to reveal a table set with small lights on it, as well as three covered plates. At the end of the table, facing to the side, was a Sekaran wearing gaudy golden robes. He had long hair, tied back with a purple hair tie. He stood when Anais entered.

"Ah, my guest," the Sekaran said. It was the voice she heard when she was eavesdropping.

The two guards bowed. "Warlord."

So she'd been correct in her assumptions. It was good to get the confirmation of her thoughts.

"At ease."

They righted themselves, one prodding Anais with the end of his laser-repeater to push her forward.

Anais moved toward the table. The room was very open, with a transparent view of the stars all around them, moving at incredible speeds, streaking across the sky in brilliant fashion. It made for a breathtaking view. On the back wall were several cabinets with artifacts in display cases: pottery, a large plate, what looked to be some sort of blade weapon, a feathered garment.

"My collection. I try to find the most exquisite item to remind me of worlds I've conquered by the time I've moved on. I brought them here. Do you like them?"

Hearing what the items represented made Anais' stomach churn. She recalled the devastation the Sekarans left on her world, and could only imagine what the retreating soldiers must have stolen from Deklyn. "They're...interesting."

"That they are. Each has a delightful story. But we are here to dine. Will you join me?"

Anais turned to see him motioning to a seat facing outward toward the stars, adjacent to him. Not having much choice, Anais took a seat.

Zebee came through the doors, greeted by the guards and Redell. He lowered his head toward Anais. "Hello again," he said, before taking seating himself.

Anger welled in Anais. How dare Zebee act as if nothing had happened. She was shot by one of his men! She found herself clenching her fists, but she wouldn't get any information if she were hostile toward them.

"I apologize for any misunderstandings," Redell said. He snapped his fingers, and a servant came forward to remove the coverings from all the plates.

The dish in front of Anais appeared to be a small portion of meat, with some yellow bean substance and sliced vegetables. She couldn't be sure what they were or what world they were from. The meal had a spiced smell to it, one that reminded her of some of the food she'd tried on Konsin II.

"My people are fairly jumpy because there's too much at stake to have any potential leaks or spies. Nevertheless, I assure you, you are a guest here, please eat."

Anais stared at the food, unsure.

"It's not poison. Please." Redell motioned an open palm toward her.

Zebee gripped the utensils with suction cups at the ends of their stems, which held the food firmly in place and began to eat. He didn't seem to have a problem. Redell joined in eating soon after. Anais stared at her food for a moment longer, but her stomach was rumbling. She hadn't eaten at the station transient bar, and it had been several hours, at least.

If they wanted to kill her, they could have already. She picked up her utensils, cut a piece of the meat, and took a bite of it. The food was delicate, melting in her mouth, very well done. Redell wasn't messing around with his culinary appetites, but why did he share it with her?

"I'm sure you're very confused right now," Redell said, as if reading her thoughts. He set his fork down, eyes boring into her. "You should know that my people are not all one united front. Different warlords have different ways of running our fiefdoms. Yes, we fight against the Elorian infidels as one, but each of our domains is fairly autonomous. I run my empire rather differently than many of my compatriots, but that's neither here nor there."

Anais watched, saying nothing. She didn't know how the Sekaran empire was split up and didn't much care.

"I find a lot of fighting to be short-sighted," Redell said. "Sometimes it's necessary, but we can all gain if we work together economically, you see. I'm sure there's much going through your mind, believing that the group that approached you was deceptive. They were not."

"The stories we told about our world being ravaged by Sekarans is very true," Zebee said. "As I'm sure is the story of your world."

And yet here you are working with them, Anais thought.

"Eltu is both strong and merciful as a prophet of the true God. I've read into the scriptures written by his divine prophet, and I'm certain I'm on the right course. You see, the conversion of souls takes time. For every punishment offered, there must also be a reward for cultures who comply. It's why I came to Zebee to help him."

"And I came to know Eltu as a result. Thank you," Zebee said.

"You're quite welcome." Redell took another bite of his food, chewing several times and swallowing before continuing. "So, you see, I'm creating a network of worlds that will eventually come into the service of Eltu. Yours will, as well—it's only a matter of time."

"I doubt it," Anais said, unable to restrain herself any longer. She seethed but tried to keep her expression flat.

"Of course you do. That's natural at first. But we have means by which to fix your outlook," Redell said.

"What do you want from me?" Anais asked.

"I understand you were eavesdropping on our conversation," Redell said. "You know far too much already. However, you can still act as a tool for us, a go-between for your people. I want to ensure you do as we wish, and if you do, you won't have any problems."

"I will never work for you," Anais said.

"You will. When we arrive on Arasu, you're going to undergo conditioning. Our friends have very interesting technology that does wonders for overly-aggressive minds." Redell dabbed his lips and chin with a napkin. "I had hoped we'd have a nice conversation and you'd come to an understanding so such techniques wouldn't be necessary, but there is too much fight in you. I see it now."

They were going to brainwash her. Anais tensed. She wasn't sure what their device was like, but it didn't sound pleasant at all. There was no way she'd go through with it, but she couldn't do anything now. She was trapped on this ship—and soon, it sounded as if she'd be trapped on Arasu. If only she had Drin with her. He'd be able to get them out of this mess. But she didn't. She was alone.

"Good. You understand," Redell said. He motioned to her food. "Please, eat. Your meal will be getting cold, and we can't have that. The chef worked so hard to prepare this delightful dish."

Anais wasn't hungry, but she knew she would need her strength later. She sat through the rest of the meal in silence as Redell and Zebee discussed trade, politics, and a hidden Sekaran outpost on Arasu. Drin warned about the world. He would want to know this information, but how could she get it to him?

Eventually, the guards returned to take her to her quarters.

Redell stood. "I hope you enjoyed our time together. It's been enlightening to me. I look forward to your people joining those in the chorus of praise of Eltu."

Anais wanted to spit at him, but she had to remain calm. Now wasn't the time to fight.

The guards kept silent afterward, closing the door on her and locking her in the room. Anais tried to pry at the door, but to no avail. She could form a light sword and cut through it, but she'd lose her advantage if the Sekarans found out about her abilities too early. She had to wait for the right time to escape.

She wished there were a way to communicate with the outside world. If only she could get a message to Drin or Elaym somehow.

Anais sighed, falling back on her cot. She was stuck, and despite her trying to work out what was going on here, she didn't have much of a plan. This Sekaran was much smarter and much more conniving than the others she had met. His way probably would be able to overtake dozens of worlds without bloodshed. She imagined Eltu-worshiping worlds generations from now, trapped because of decisions a few ambassadors made to try to boost the economies of war-torn worlds. Every decision they made had consequences for the future, even hers.

The thoughts weighed on Anais as if something heavy landed atop her. The stress tightened her temples and gave her a headache. For now, there was nothing she could do. She closed her eyes.

FIFTEEN

Laser fire engulfed the cave. Bright lights shone everywhere. Bolts bounced off Drin's nanite shielding, ricocheting into the cave walls. Rocks and dust flew, providing a smokescreen for him and Err-dio.

"Run!" Drin said.

Err-dio took back off the direction they'd come. "Where do we go? We can't head to the cavern."

"Go the other direction," Drin said. He formed his light sword, slashing at a Sekaran who came too close. The others in the enemy unit weren't so brazen, staying back and continuing their rapid fire.

Drin's shield held, but its power was diminishing. He wouldn't be able to hold forever in close quarters. Hopefully, Err-dio managed to get enough of a head start to not risk getting hit.

He turned and followed Err-dio deeper into the cave. They returned to the hexagonal walls, this time, taking the leftmost path. Drin caught up to Err-dio quickly, but the Sekarans were right on his heels. He stopped and turned to run the other direction.

As he'd hoped, the Sekarans' momentum carried them

forward, and they couldn't adjust to stay back quickly enough to evade Drin.

He sliced at three of the Sekarans, who fell when his blade struck true. It caused the others to take pause and back up. There were too many of them to fight like this. He wouldn't be able to hold them off forever, especially if they brought reinforcements.

Having space again gave Drin time to think as he backed his way in the direction Err-dio ran. He had to slow them somehow. Otherwise his shields would eventually fail.

The cave shortened as he moved, the roof barely above his head in some spots. It gave Drin an idea.

He raised his light sword, driving it into the rocks above him. As he continued backward, he flung his blade wildly. The cave ceiling rumbled and began to collapse. Drin let his light sword dissipate and hurried backward faster.

Rocks and dirt fell at an incredible rate, piling where he had stood a moment prior. It didn't completely cut off the way, but it would make it difficult for the Sekarans to follow.

Satisfied with his work, Drin turned and jogged to catch up with Err-dio again. He found his companion after a couple of minutes of running.

"You dispatched the entire unit?" Err-dio asked, wide-eyed with amazement.

"I slowed them down. Hopefully, this path leads somewhere. Otherwise we're trapped."

Err-dio and Drin slowed their pace to a walk as they continued through the small corridor. As they traveled, it opened wider until it became a large enough of a lane for vehicles to be able to get through. It kept getting bigger and split off in three different directions this time.

"Which way do we go?" Err-dio asked.

"Let's stay toward the middle," Drin said.

They kept walking, and the corridor kept getting bigger. It

eventually opened to the point where Drin could see light trickling through a closed metal door. Drin opened the door to reveal a large area, hollowed out, with rock pillars at least five stories high held up a rock overhang. And it needed it. Several buildings were constructed in the rock face. A whole city built into the cliff, covered by the rock overhang, facing the world outside.

Most of the buildings were made of stone bricks, some connected with the rock face itself, holding up the heavy ceiling. Vehicles moved through the streets, along with a smattering of insectoid creatures—Arasu's natives. They didn't pay Drin or Err-dio any heed at first, busy with their work. There was no sign of any Sekaran presence.

"This is an incredible feat of engineering," Err-dio said.

"Mm," Drin agreed. It was good they took this path, a blessing from God. The lack of Sekarans here was another blessing. Perhaps the enemy operated separately than the local populace. It meant they had a chance to try to accomplish something rather than go on the run. "Let's see if we can find an interstellar comm unit."

"Reinforcements," Err-dio said. "Wise."

"The Lord never asked his followers to do battle alone. We are meant to work together for His will." It was something Drin realized after he'd defected from his unit months ago. He'd repented for his misdeeds, and he hoped the Lord would bless his efforts now.

He made his way to the closest local he could find, one who recoiled at the sight of Drin and his six-armed companion. They must have looked like very strange aliens to the people here. "Do you speak basic?" Drin asked.

"I do," the Arasu said. "You're not from here."

"Indeed, I am not," Drin said. "My companion and I were working on diplomatic relations with your world, and we have become lost. Is there an interstellar comm available for public use somewhere nearby?"

"I've never had use for such things." The Arasu twitched several times.

Drin wasn't sure if it was a natural part of this being's physiology. It would be best not to draw attention to it.

"Ah," the Arasu said after a brief pause. "I'm informed there is one three streets down and to your left. A large stone door on the corner."

"Thank you kindly," Drin said, bowing his head. There was the possibility the Arasu were hostile, and the information he provided was suspect, but Drin had done all he could to act as if there were nothing out of the ordinary. Would the alien betray him? But he still had to go where the Arasu indicated. It wasn't as if he had much choice on this foreign world with no way to contact others.

Drin led Err-dio in the direction the Arasu told them, stopping before several buildings that matched the description. These creatures didn't have much of a propensity for differing architecture. It was very easy to mistake one building for another. They had signage with hexagons burnt into the buildings, but little to differentiate them otherwise.

"I think the kind fellow meant this one," Err-dio said, pointing toward a stone door up three steps.

"We can at least try." Drin ascended the steps and approached the door. He wasn't sure what the local customs would be here. If this were a public place, most worlds would allow admittance without announcing oneself, but there were some where it could be a fatal error to trespass. It would be better to err on the side of caution. He knocked on the big stone door.

Another Arasu opened the door, looking similar to the one Drin had met prior. He could hardly tell them apart. Their styles blended into the scenery, almost like they wanted to hide within the city, and their meager clothing all looked the same.

"What's the racket?" the Arasu asked.

"I was pointed this direction by a kind fellow who said there's an interstellar comm device here," Drin said.

"There is."

"May I use it?"

"Who are you?"

"My name is Drin."

"Drin. I haven't heard of you." The Arasu moved to close the door.

Drin held up a hand. "Please. We are travelers here on a diplomatic mission, and we're lost. I need to contact my people."

The Arasu twitched like the other had before. He paused. And then he held the door open. "Only one has interacted with you. Very strange for someone on a diplomatic mission, but he says you appear harmless. Come in."

Drin and Err-dio entered into the building. It had several rows of computer terminals set up, along with seats at them. A few Arasu occupied some of the terminals.

"We allow communication here in service to our queen, but you may call your people." The Arasu who greeted them motioned to an empty terminal.

Drin sat at the computer. The display had strange hexagonal patterns like much of the Arasu world. "Can you pull up a display in basic?"

The Arasu appeared annoyed with him, but he jutted out his arm and made the display shift. Drin could read the words now, and it appeared much like any other comm terminal he'd used before.

"I need to get back to work," the Arasu said, leaving them without waiting for a reply.

"He was short with you," Err-dio said.

"Just busy, but he gave us what we needed. We should be thankful."

"Praise Yezuah," Err-dio said.

Drin nodded and tried to enter in the comm codes he recalled from memory. Most of the Templars he'd interacted with in recent years were from the *Justicar*. There was one emergency frequency used for contacting the mother church.

The comm device connected, shifting star patterns on a waiting screen. When it reached someone within the church, the display flickered and displayed an image of a green man with a red frock and a golden necklace with the Writ of Peace, symbolizing the document that brought accord to all of the twelve tribes of Eloria. Only cardinals in the church were given such necklaces. Drin recognized the round face and droopy eyes before him as Cardinal Levy.

Drin bowed his head as best he could. "Cardinal," he said.

"Rise, my son. And who might I have the pleasure of speaking with?" Cardinal Levy's eyes flicked from Drin to Err-dio and back again.

"I am Drin, Templar of the *Justicar*, and this—"

"*Justicar*? The ship that was just destroyed by the Sekaran ambush?"

"The same," Drin said.

"Terrible. Though we'd sent a team to survey the wreckage after we were sure the Sekarans departed, we found no survivors."

"The Sekarans were ruthless. I was lucky. The asteroid debris field concealed my viper, and I was able to shut down power and evade their search teams."

"We are blessed to still have you among our people."

"Thank you," Drin said.

"And who's your companion?"

Err-dio stepped forward and bowed his head. "I am Err-dio of the free Skree people, squire to Templar Drin."

"Very good," Cardinal Levy said. "I'm getting coordinates that you're on a world called Arasu. It's pretty far into the Tertia Spiral Arm. How did you get out there?"

Drin explained his situation after the crash, how he'd heard about the Sekaran superweapon, and how he intercepted some of their communications. "It's a strange world, and they appear to be building another weapon here."

"You wish I should dispatch the fleet? They were going to try to intercept the Sekarans who destroyed your vessel to bring the heretics to justice. I—"

Drin turned as the door to the place opened. "I'm going to have to go. Please send reinforcements as fast as possible," he said. He formed his armor and his light sword. Laser-repeater bolts flew in his direction.

The terminal sparked, shorting out. Its display shattered, causing a panic among the Arasu in the room. Err-dio ducked backward.

At the door stood four Sekaran soldiers, and they advanced on Drin.

SIXTEEN

Anais awoke to her door opening. One of the Arasu stepped inside, this one unarmed. The door closed behind the creature.

She sat up quickly, not sure what the creature wanted. The Arasu didn't appear to be making any moves toward her, but she still reacted with the fight instinct, not wanting to be put in a position where she would be abused by another alien.

"I'm sorry to startle you," the Arasu said. "My name is Drezzie. I've been watching what's going on since you've arrived here."

"Why?" Anais asked. She pressed her hands down on the bed, trying to force herself to be calm.

Drezzie glanced over his shoulder, as if someone might come into the room and spot him here at any moment. "I want you to know that not all of my people are bowing to the Sekarans. Some do, and they're influential, but there are those of us who are trying to resist what they're doing on our world."

"They said they're going to reeducate me somehow."

"A brain scramble," Drezzie said.

That didn't sound appealing at all. "Can you help me escape? Not now, but when we get to your world?" Anais asked.

Drezzie nodded. "I can, but I'm not sure it will do any good. You'll be very easy to spot in a world full of my people. We don't have many outsider visitors because our weather can become very harsh depending on the cycle time."

"I think if I can get away and hide somewhere, I can manage myself."

"Perhaps I can contact some of the others and see if they'd be willing to harbor and assist you. We haven't done anything like this before."

Even though it was hard to read Arasu expressions, Anais could tell Drezzie was afraid. Even coming to her at all was a risk. What if she told the warlord of this insurrection? The Sekarans would shut it down quickly. He had very little reason to trust her, yet poured it on her all the same. This was her opportunity to do some good and help. "I would appreciate it. And I'll do my best to help your world."

"Thank you," he said. "We're not the only ones. Many in the coalition wouldn't be happy if they knew the Sekarans were trying to manipulate our worlds."

"I'm sure that's the case," Anais said. "Do you know where we're going to land? Are there a lot of people around?"

"It'll be one of our cities, which we build into caverns and rock faces to protect it from the elements. You will both be in open space and confined at the same time—it's hard to describe without you seeing it."

"I appreciate the information," Anais said.

The doors opened, and guards arrived again. They had a covered meal for her this time.

"What are you doing here?" one of the guards asked Drezzie.

Drezzie stiffened. "I wanted to see our guest. I had never seen an off-worlder of this kind before."

The guard huffed. "You would do well to satiate your curiosity by looking at holovids," he said, stepping forward and delivering the tray to a side table adjacent to Anais. "Here is your next meal."

"No more dining with the warlord?" Anais asked.

"He is busy," the guard said. He turned and motioned his companions toward the exit. They followed, including Drezzie, who seemed to spare a last glance for Anais before the door closed.

That was an odd encounter, but a useful one. If she had someone who was truly willing to help her, she might be able to get a message out to Drin or Elaym. No matter what happened to her, she needed to get Deklyn out of this trade agreement. Her world couldn't get tied up with the Sekarans again.

The hope made her wait much less dreadful than it had been. She didn't want to have to find out exactly how a brain scrambler worked. She could only imagine the horrors others endured from such a device. Most worlds made such coercion tactics illegal, but the Sekarans weren't ones for scruples.

She hoped Drezzie was honest. It occurred to her that he might have been sent in to get information from her. But he hadn't asked her many questions, just offered her help, hadn't he?

After being betrayed by the Arasu in the first place, Anais wasn't so sure she could trust another one. But she had no other choice, did she? No one else knew of her captivity, and soon, she would be on a foreign world without any friends.

The thought made Anais shiver. But she had gotten herself into this mess—again. This time, she felt like she'd taken a responsible path, but it still didn't matter. Why did she always end up captured by Sekarans?

Perhaps this was part of God's plan. Drin would view it as such. She was placed here for a reason.

Anais closed her eyes and took a deep breath. If she wanted to have the presence of mind of Drin in these situations, she needed to act more like him. She quieted her mind and began to pray.

SEVENTEEN

The Sekarans shot up the room, causing complete chaos. Laser bolts seemed to come from everywhere, hitting computers, people, and the walls indiscriminately. The Sekarans took no care for the Arasu civilians present.

Drin knew from experience they didn't care about local populations. The poor race of this planet had been duped into serving these evil masters, just like he had seen on so many other worlds.

The blasts kept coming, and Drin kept strafing through the room. He'd flipped several tables with comm terminals over, creating a barrier, cover for the local populace—and more importantly, Err-dio—to hide behind. So far, they seemed to be safe, as the Sekarans focused fire on him.

Having had very little time to meditate, eat, or rest, Drin's nanites were already strained from the prior battle in the cave. They needed time to recover, and so did he, but he didn't have the luxury of time. He had to remove the threat first.

Several blasts hit him, his nanite shield flickering. It still held at slightly over eighty percent power. Several civilians who had been hit writhed on the floor in pain. Others screamed.

Drin clutched his light sword, turning toward the Sekarans. He pivoted, bent his knees, and leaped toward them.

It didn't make quite the display that it would have had he been outside. The ceiling precluded him from jumping too high, but it managed to cause the Sekarans to flinch all the same. The second of reprieve was all Drin needed to launch into one of the Sekaran gunmen. He drove his light sword through the Sekaran's belly, energy protruding out the back of him.

The Sekaran choked, dropped his gun, and then fell to the floor.

Drin kicked the laser-repeater behind him, toward the barrier of desks he'd set up by knocking them over. He hoped Err-dio was still behind the tables, and that he could see what Drin was doing. There was no way to call out to him without drawing Sekaran attention, and they would roast Err-dio when he came out from hiding if they knew Drin was intentionally giving him a weapon.

Instead, Drin tried to make the enemy focus on him. He charged toward another one of the Sekarans, who dodged out of the way of his blows.

Drin had made a mistake in over-committing. His back was faced to the enemy, and the three of them turned on him, firing. Several close-range shots cut into his shielding power again. He was taking too many hits in too short of a span. The confined nature of his last battle in the cave, and now in this room, were taking a toll on him. He much preferred to be out in open space where he could leap around at will and use cover to do his work.

He spun, swinging his energy blade in a wide-angle. It clipped the Sekaran, who had just dodged his last blow, cutting him with surface-level wounds across his arms and chest. Drin lunged and drew his light sword back the opposite direction. The fluid movements were too much for the Sekaran to handle. Having a non-physical weapon had its advantages, as Drin didn't have to worry about weight or resistances as he would with a real blade.

Two Sekarans remained.

One had crept up behind Drin and kicked him in the back.

Drin hadn't been expecting the assault. He lost his balance and fell face-first to the floor. His visor smacked against the hard tile, the jolt sending reverberations down Drin's spine. He winced, trying to will the pain away.

The Sekaran placed his weight on Drin, pinning him down with a boot. He kept firing laser bolts at Drin's head through the process.

Drin flailed with his light sword, but the Sekaran managed to dance around the swing of the blade.

The second Sekaran stepped into Drin's field of vision, also firing shots at Drin's head. The nanite shield power drained. He couldn't take many more shots like this. These soldiers had his number. Drin muttered a prayer for deliverance and for forgiveness of sins, in case this would be the end of him.

Then, the Sekaran who pinned him down stumbled backward. Several more shots rang out, but not at Drin's head.

Drin rolled over to try to get a better view, and to get himself out of the blasts of the other soldier.

The one who had held him down had several holes in him from laser bolts. Drin glanced back over his shoulder.

Err-dio had taken the laser-repeater, setting up aim from behind the desk where he'd been hiding. He used the edge of the desk to steady his aim, shooting with far greater accuracy than the Sekarans had.

The second Sekaran took several hits to the chest, collapsing along with his companion.

The room quieted, no more laser fire erupting. Some of the surviving Arasu muttered to each other.

Drin pushed himself to his feet and looked to Err-dio. "We should be getting out of here."

"I couldn't agree with you more," Err-dio said.

The Arasu started to recover their senses, though the man who had ushered them in lay in a pool of his blood on the floor. It was pure chaos. Drin didn't have time to bring peace to these poor people. He stepped to the door, opening it, and ushering Err-dio go through.

Outside, Arasu walked through the streets unaware, but no Sekarans appeared to be coming to back up their fellow soldiers. They were in the clear for now.

Drin made his way into a shaded area, covered by rock face, and out of the shine of several of the street lights, as the sun had appeared to have set into the evening time. He wasn't sure the area would conceal them any better from these creatures' eyes than the lit areas. Judging from the way everything was constructed, and all the hexagonal insets in the caves, which mirrored the look of their current architecture, these creatures developed as cave dwellers, probably even burrowers.

An alarm sounded in the city. It rang out through the streets, echoing because of all the rock faces. The sound pierced Drin's ears, inescapable. It pulsed in quick intervals.

"They must be sounding a warning for us," Err-dio said. He clutched his newfound laser-repeater. "Where should we make our stand?"

"Wait," Drin said.

Several of the creatures scurried through the streets. They didn't appear to be searching for them at all. Instead, they ran to the different structures. Some stood at the doors, ushering the others in, but all of the people seemed to be in a panic.

"I don't think this has to do with us," Drin said.

He focused on his nanites, using their sensors to spot other spectrums to try to enhance his senses. Something rumbled at a low level, drowned out by the alarm sounds. Drin willed his helmet to stop letting him hear the frequencies of the alarm. The rumbling grew louder, coming toward them. "We're not safe here," Drin said.

He hustled down the street. Err-dio followed. Most of the doors had been sealed shut. Drin took note of the construction of the buildings now. They were built into the rock face, and they were sealed airtight. It wasn't just some fluke of design, this was done for a purpose.

Out of the corner of his eye, he could see the cause of the sound. A giant wave of water poured through the canyon just beyond the city. It headed toward them, and it was coming quickly.

"Get into one of the structures!" Drin shouted. He spun to face the growing water in the distance. It moved at tremendous speeds. They had very little time.

Err-dio moved to one that had just closed. He pounded his fists on the door. It opened, and the creatures pulled Err-dio inside.

Drin ran over to the door, but the water edged up behind him, building into a giant wave.

"I'm sorry! No time!" the Arasu said. It shut as Drin reached the door. He placed his hands on it, but it was sealed. He was too late.

Drin turned to face the wave. He had his armor, his nanites. Though water was the natural enemy of machines, these could resist it, couldn't they?

He'd never faced a situation where he'd be pummeled by water. He did his best to keep his balance, willing as much weight into his legs as the nanites could muster. They could create suction for zero-G situations, surely they could hold him in place here.

The water filled the cavern, a wall of blue and white rushing toward Drin. It slammed into him, the sheer force of it like he'd been hit with a troop transport carrier. At first, he was able to maintain his balance, but the water kept gushing across him, pelting his body. The nanites didn't have the power remaining in them to be able to keep suction with the street.

The wave rushed Drin away, sweeping him up in its incredible current. He spun backward and couldn't right himself, struggling not to flip end-over-end as the water carried him. He could hardly see what was going on around him, it moved so quickly. He heard a *crack*. His neck snapped back against something hard and solid. He'd hit a wall.

His power meter blinked red. It was too much strain for the nanites. The armor wasn't going to last much longer. Drin did his best to take deep breaths. The nanites stored air for him as best they could. Hopefully, these flash floods didn't last too long. He would need to recover soon.

Another current caught him in its stream, pulling him deeper into the cave structure beyond the city. Drin's head slammed into a wall.

This time, he lost consciousness.

EIGHTEEN

Anais stood in one of the main cargo holds of the vessel, waiting for the ship to land and for a ramp to open to the outside world. Guards and workers surrounded her and the two men with her—Zebee and Warlord Redell. She hadn't seen Drezzie since he'd been in her quarters several hours ago, and she wondered if he was going to come through with some sort of escape plan for them.

Zebee held a hand to his ear as if listening to a comm. "I see. How long is the delay going to be? Yes. It won't be a problem. Thank you for informing me."

Redell cocked his head at Zebee, concerned. "Is something the matter with our landing?"

"We're experiencing a slight delay because of a flash flood in the Dubu Holding. It will recede in a few minutes, nothing to worry about," Zebee said.

Redell smiled at Anais. "It's a fascinating world once you get to know Arasu. I'm sure it's quite exciting for you. You'll love this little world even more after you're conditioned for us," he said.

He was so callous about brain scrambling. How did these

Sekarans all seem to get this way, to where they could disregard sentient life? She recalled they didn't view other creatures as entirely sentient. At least until they converted. She was just an infidel to them, disposable for their purposes.

"Why is this world so important to you?" she asked. "It didn't look very appealing from the maps I saw during the trade agreement. Zebee doesn't have many resources to work with" It might have been too obvious a ploy to get information, but she needed something.

"I don't suppose there's any harm in obliging your question," Redell said. "You see, we discovered a cache of ancient devices which came from an ancient race. It seems the Arasu were not the first creatures to inhabit this world. There's legends of Arasu gods which are quite interesting, but I'll keep the story short."

He paced in front of her, staring out toward the closed ramp as if in thought. "These ancient aliens—or gods—had technology far beyond what we could comprehend. Our scientists discovered them when we first came to Arasu, before our military forces were repelled. It's been a priority to come back and analyze these devices, long buried by the sands of time."

"Redell came to us with offers of trade. He wanted access to our weapons, and he would help us with materials to fortify our cities from our flash floods," Zebee said.

Redell nodded. "Indeed. And it's saved the lives of many Arasu. They will be more grateful in time, after the wounds of our prior occupation are erased from their history. Regardless, we were able to uncover some of these devices and began to experiment with them."

"Like you did with Konsin II," Anais said. She snapped her jaw shut, realizing she probably had revealed too much.

"You've heard of it, then? I suppose news spreads quickly when destruction of that magnitude occurs. Yes, that was one of the devices we uncovered. It directs energy at a planet core, causing it to simmer with pressure until it finally explodes like a star going nova. Very interesting, and useful as a weapon, though dangerous."

"You killed a lot of people," Anais said.

"Not me." Redell shook his head. "Others who are short-sighted. But the device needed to be tested, nonetheless. There are far more treasures buried on Arasu. We're trying to uncover what they are and what they do, but much of the alien language and processes are so far beyond us. It's difficult."

This was a lot of information for Anais to process. Ancient aliens and technologies? It was far beyond her abilities to know what to do about it. It sounded like this had big implications for a galactic scale. She needed Drin here.

The ship landed. Its gates opened. A ramp descended to an outside world which looked barren, with a rock wall obscuring the view of anything else. Everything appeared to be damp in the area. The air smelled of moisture, like after a fresh rain.

"Time to go," Redell said, motioning ahead of him.

To where? Her unasked question was answered when they stepped forward. The rock face had been carved out from the bottom, with a number of small structures etched into it. A city within this giant rock wall. All of the faces of the buildings were just as wet as everything else around them. The city looked vacant, though as Anais descended the ramp, more of the Arasu bug-creatures came out of their structures.

A laser-repeater powered up with a buzz behind her. Anais turned.

Drezzie stood behind her group, along with an armed team. "Turn over the Deklyn woman," he said.

Redell turned, a glint in his eye, which showed he enjoyed this all too much. He produced a laser-repeater of his own, drawing it with incredible speed. He shot Drezzie directly in the chest.

All hell broke loose, the warlord's guards firing, and the rebels shooting as well. The Arasu guards moved for cover on both sides, trying to utilize different portions of the cargo bay. It appeared the Sekaran loyalists had a slight numbers advantage, but the element of surprise evened the fight quickly.

Anais stood in the crossfire, though no one was aiming for her. Now was the time for her to act. She concentrated on her nanites, forming armor and shielding around her.

Redell recoiled, hopping over the side of the ramp to hide. "The woman is a witch! She has Elorian magic! Kill her!"

His guards turned to her, focusing their fire on her as she lingered in the open. Anais' shields managed to absorb the blast. She formed a light sword in her hand. It was still awkward for her, even though Drin had spent considerable time training her.

Here goes nothing.

Laser-repeater bolts pelted her shielding, causing Anais to stumble backward. How did Drin take hits and keep himself so poised? She recalled his words of wisdom. Fighting was all about balance, maintaining yours and throwing your opponent off simultaneously.

Anais widened her stance and carefully looked for targets. It appeared as if there were two Sekaran guards, flanked by several Arasu, who fought on their behalf.

The Sekarans would be her immediate targets. Anais bolted toward one of them, using all of the speed her Deklyn physique and nanites provided. Her momentum pushed her faster than the Sekarans anticipated, their shots firing into the deck behind her. She held her light sword to the side, like a clothesline, and she ran, intending to push past the Sekaran.

It worked. She was only slowed by the resistance of her light sword piercing flesh. It cut through the Sekaran closest to her. The soldier cried in pain before he drew no further breath. Anais turned to another target, not wanting to see what she'd done to the body. It made her wince thinking about it. She'd killed before in battle, but this time felt different, like she was more of an aggressor than fighting out of desperate need.

She had to clear her mind.

Easier said than done.

Laser bolts struck her back shielding, interrupting her thoughts and making her stumble again.

She turned. One Sekaran guard left. Redell had disappeared from sight. Had the warlord fled?

Anais dodged the next round of blasts coming from the Arasu. The resistance stopped some of their fire by picking off two of them, giving Anais time to focus on the Sekaran.

Her enemy spotted her, backpedaling. Anais grinned, thinking of how she could instill fear into the hearts of Sekarans. It felt good, after having lived in fear of them for so long, helpless as both she and her world were enslaved. They would pay.

She pressed forward, and though the Sekaran turned and started running away from her, he was no match for her speed. Guilt welled in her as she drove her light sword through his back. He had no chance.

Flesh sizzled as the Sekaran collapsed to his knees. Anais pulled the blade out again. Was this how Drin felt when he killed these soldiers so easily? Even in recent battles, she couldn't help but sense an uneasiness from him.

Much like her, he hated killing. Still, she hated Sekarans more than the deed. If she could purge the universe of more of them... It wasn't a kind thought, but she could never forgive them for all the devastation they'd caused her world.

Anais turned back to the battle. The Sekaran-loyal line had broken, allowing the resisting Arasu to break through. One came to her and hooked her by the arm. "Let's go. We have to get you to our resistance leader."

"Okay," Anais said.

The Arasu pulled her in one direction and let her go. Anais

kept pace with him. They traversed through the city, which had several puddles and damp areas, which the Arasu evaded. All of the structures looked much the same as one another, making it very difficult for Anais to determine their location.

At least they'd escaped the Sekaran warlord. She'd evaded his brain scrambling—for now. No doubt, he would be sending search parties for her, and if she stayed in the open, she'd be found. "I hope we're not being followed," Anais said as she ran through the city with the Arasu she'd just met.

"I'm taking a circuitous route," he said.

They weaved through similar buildings until they came to an area of the cave, which was much darker than where they'd parked the ship. They slipped past some of the structures into a little crack in the back rock face, which she had to slide through sideways to make it inside. From there, they traveled through a long opening, much the same width the entire way through. It was tight in spots, and difficult to get through. After a time, it opened up into a much more normal-sized corridor.

"I'm sorry for the difficult travel, but keeping hidden is the best way for our people to keep safe."

Anais wanted to mention that it was a good way to get them trapped, but she figured it would be best to leave it be for now.

The corridor was covered in hollow hexagons, much like the artificial ones that lined the ship she'd been captured on. Dust settled in them, as if they'd been there for a long time. Anais couldn't resist the urge to touch the surface, which was hard as a rock.

"Our people worked in hives for a very long time. We stored food in these combs before we learned to function in the cities outside," the Arasu said, seeming to take note of her curiosity.

"Interesting," Anais said, glancing around. It was an amazing amount of work to make these combs and that they still remained intact...for how long? She was sure this world had just as interesting a history as Deklyn.

The corridor opened into a much larger cave, where several Arasu stood guard. Others worked on tablets, while still others lounged about. All of their beady, bug eyes turned to Anais when they entered.

"I brought us a guest," Anais's guide announced.

A few of the Arasu muttered greetings.

One stood and moved to stand in front of her. "Hello, my name is Cudree. For all intents and purposes, I am the queen here. It's not a perfect translation to basic for my position, but it will do for now."

Anais bowed her head in respect. "I'm Anais, from Deklyn."

Her guide turned to her. "I'm Fardree. Drezzie spoke very highly of you. He believed you might be the catalyst we need for change in these parts."

"Change?" Anais asked.

"We want the Sekarans off our world permanently," Cudree said. "We've been building our resources and biding our time for the right moment. It looks like the moment has come. We're going to start a revolution."

NINETEEN

Drin coughed, choking up some water he'd inhaled. He was soaked. Some of the water had seeped through his nanite armor. He was slumped against one of the rear walls of the cave, alone. Some of the Arasu had come out of their hiding places, but it didn't seem as if any of them had taken notice of him.

He willed the nanites to convert into energy. Their heat would dry him much more quickly than any other means. He'd blacked out from the force of the current, which had pushed him around like a rag doll. It was amazing he'd survived. The grace of God. *You always keep me alive. For a purpose, don't you?* Drin asked, though no answer came from Yezuah. He shook his head, lifting himself to his feet.

What he needed to do was rest, meditate, lie down, have some food—anything to give himself a break from the relentless fighting as of late.

"Drin!" a voice said from further into the cave.

He shifted his vision to infrared so he could see who was coming toward him. He spotted the six-arms of the Skree. "Err-dio," Drin said.

"We thought we'd lost you. My new friends told me no one could survive one of the flash floods. The Arasu have a broadcast warning system that transmits to their antennae on a frequency we cannot hear." Err-dio motioned behind him to two Arasu who followed him. "Let's get you back to their place. They are very kind people. They fed me and gave me hot tea."

Drin nodded at them. "Thank you very much for your hospitality," he said.

"It's no problem. What you've done just by living through this is a miracle. How—?"

"By the grace of God," Drin said.

"God?" the Arasu asked.

"I'll tell you about Him on the way."

Drin did his best to relay the story of creation, of Yezuah and his followers, and the promises he'd made to return on the day of the last battle. He made clear that belief in Yezuah was all that was required to attain salvation. They didn't have too much time to absorb the information, though, because they reached the Arasu accommodations.

Inside, the Arasu gave Drin a towel and provided him with hot tea, just as they had told Err-dio they would. They were inquisitive, asking more questions about Yezuah, Drin, and where he was from. The Sekarans hadn't poisoned the Arasu about the Elorians as they had many other worlds. The people here were naive, not knowing much of the outside universe. They were in awe of Drin and Err-dio.

"And Drin used Yezuah's miraculous technology to help liberate my world from Sekarans," Err-dio said.

The two Arasu visibly tensed.

"I'm sorry, do you like Sekarans?" Err-dio asked.

The male shook his head. "No, they took our son from us."

The female slumped her shoulders. "We fear them. If we

speak ill of them they will come for us. Let's not speak of them anymore."

"Very well," Err-dio said.

"The same technology allowed me to survive your flash flood," Drin said. "It was very close. I think if the water would have continued for even a minute longer, I might have drowned," Drin said.

"Well, it is good you didn't. We'll leave you be for now. Please, eat and be comfortable. You can stay here as long as you need," the female Arasu said.

The two Arasu left to tend to their house, and Drin and Err-dio sat alone.

"I was frightened you wouldn't make it," Err-dio said, "but I prayed for your safety the entire time."

"Thank you," Drin said.

The Arasu returned with food from their market. Drin shared the meal with them, grateful for the first sustenance he'd had since arriving on this world. He'd been going so hard for so long, he'd nearly forgotten the basic necessities of life. With the nanites, he could push himself a lot longer than most people could, but there was always a breaking point.

His nanites needed rest and recovery as much as he did. They'd been pushed to their maximum with the flash flood. Err-dio meeting these Arasu had been a gift from God, exactly the reprieve he needed.

"If you don't mind, I'd like some time to meditate," Drin said. "It may sound strange, but it's a part of my religion."

The two Arasu looked at each other and then to Drin. They pointed to a back room. "You can have peace and quiet in there."

"Thank you so much for your hospitality. You are doing God's work," Drin said.

"Don't worry about the plates and the rest of the food. We'll clean up," the female Arasu said.

Drin nodded, stood, and headed toward the back room. He took a seat on the floor, let his shoulders relax, and closed his eyes. Err-dio continued to talk with the Arasu in the other room, giving him the time and space he needed.

It was rest he required, time to rejuvenate his nanites. It might take some time with how much they'd been overexerted, but he would need to be at full strength for whatever came next. The Sekarans would hear of his miraculous survival sooner or later, and they would send more of their numbers to come searching for him.

Drin breathed in and out slowly, letting his mind empty. *Lord Yezuah, protect me in this holy mission, guide me to the right course to be able to do your will.*

It often seemed like these battles did no good, like he moved from one fight to another, an endless stream of enemies ever nipping at his heels. But he couldn't get discouraged. The weapon he'd found in the caves here could destroy so many lives if left in Sekaran hands. He had to put a stop to their plans.

Protect the innocents here, so they may come to know you as Err-dio and I do. And bless your servants who fight in your name, especially those who have fallen.

Father Cline, Baifed, Sister Vith. He'd lost so many friends and loved ones in recent days. Was he pressing himself into action to avoid grieving? It was possible, but Drin felt his cause had more to it than that. He had work to do still.

Lord, use me as your instrument, so I may bring others into your service and they may get to know your salvation.

Truth be told, Err-dio was more effective at converting others to the gospel than Drin. He'd been able to bring many of the Skree race to the faith, but he hadn't had the same impact on Deklyn. But did it matter? Err-dio was instilling these Arasu with curiosity in Yezuah. If Drin influenced Err-dio, and he in turn influenced others, would the Lord still consider it good work he had done?

Then there was Anais. Her faith, at least, had come from him.

Please keep Anais safe. She is your daughter and trying to do your will, wherever she may be.

Drin's heart stung far more at being away from Anais than it did losing his Elorian companions. Guilt at his misplaced priorities swept over him. But he didn't worry about his dead companions—they were in Yezuah's kingdom now, finally able to have peace. Drin longed for that peace for himself. But he found it in this realm when he was with the girl.

Keep me from temptation, Lord. Help my love to stay pure and true.

If he couldn't remove his feelings entirely, he had to keep them contained.

He muttered the Lord's prayer several times to himself, until the mantra became rote, unthinking. Eventually, Drin fell asleep.

He awoke several hours later, his eyes fluttering open. Peace filled him, a rested wholeness he hadn't felt in a while. The nanites were restored to their full power.

He opened the door and stepped out into the hallway. The lights were off in the house. Err-dio had collapsed on a couch, and the Arasu were nowhere in sight. Drin stood and made his way over to where Err-dio slept. He lightly prodded the man in the shoulder.

Err-dio turned and stirred, looking up to Drin. "Templar Drin. You're done with your meditations," he said.

"And sleep," Drin confessed.

Err-dio chuckled. "I tend to fall asleep during our meditation sessions, as well. It's the middle of the night. I was happy to get some sleep myself. Is there something urgent?" His face drew into concern as he seemed to put together that this wouldn't be a social call at this hour.

"Yes. We should get moving. The longer we stay in one place, the more dangerous it is not only for us, but for those who aid us," Drin said.

Err-dio pushed himself upright into a seated position. "I was worried you'd come to that conclusion. It would have been nice to spend a few days here and take a break."

"It would have," Drin said. "But we have far more important matters to attend to."

"What's that?"

"We need to secure the superweapon in the cave. I prayed, and I have the feeling we can't wait much longer, or the Sekarans might use it and destroy some unsuspecting world."

"We can't wait for your back-up to arrive?" Err-dio asked.

"I don't know they're coming. The cardinal didn't seem too happy to speak with me."

"I can't imagine he'd leave you stranded here."

Drin shrugged. "Perhaps not, but we still have to do what we must. It may be hard, we may lose our lives, but what is that compared with the lives of billions?"

Err-dio stood and stretched. "I trust you and will follow where you lead."

Drin nodded. "I'm honored by your trust. I will not forsake it. Let's go." He made his way toward the door.

TWENTY

Anais stood in the small cavern, a makeshift headquarters for these rebel Arasu.

Cudree leaned over a makeshift map of the Arasu city. He had markers where his people were at, places the team here wanted to fortify. "I don't expect much resistance from the general populace. They don't like the Sekarans any better than we do, but many don't know what's going on, or want to turn a blind eye to the fact we're still enslaved. What we need to do is secure the emergency flash flood broadcasting tower and get the word out from there. If we can get a signal to the populace, we can create a full-scale revolt."

Anais nodded. The Arasu seemed to look to her for guidance, as if she were some kind of expert in revolutions. She'd been involved in two, but the planning had been by others. She'd just happened to been the right place at the right time in a lot of these battles. It made her uncomfortable, and also made her wish Drin was here all the more.

He'd know what to do. He'd be able to tell the Arasu whether their plans were sound or whether they were foolish. But he wasn't here. She was alone.

Anais bit her lip, looking at the maps. "What happens if the Sekarans decide to bring down the entire city with explosives?"

"Would they do such a thing?" Cudree asked. "There are innocents."

"I've never seen that stop them before," Anais said.

"We'll have to keep them out of here in totality, then. It means we'll have to seal the entrance to the cave where they're operating." Cudree motioned to a point on the map. "And also secure the river bed outside so they can't land vessels in here. I'm not sure we have the manpower to do all of this."

"There'll be some internal fighting as well, yes?" Anais asked.

She considered. There were some abilities and powers she had which could help. When Drin found himself outmatched, he brought down an entire building on top of one of the Sekaran battlemages. She might be able to do the same in the cave. "I think I'd be best in a confined space. I have technology I can use to help seal the tunnels so the Sekarans can't get through. You'll not have to send as many men, because I'll be able to handle it."

"Are you certain?"

Anais nodded.

"Then we'll do it. I'll send Fardree with you, and two others. I was going to send a whole unit in case the Sekarans flood through. Will it be enough?"

"I think so," Anais said. She wished she'd sounded more confident, but she wasn't sure of her abilities, even now. She found herself biting her bottom lip out of nervous habit.

"It will have to do for now. We'll need a good amount of people at the cave opening." Cudree sighed. "I'm not sure we have the power to do this."

"We'll have to have faith that this is the right course. Are there even that many Sekarans on the planet? I didn't see many when we ran through the city," Anais said.

"They're concentrated in the deep caves. The warlord's strategy is to not let the general population know they're still being manipulated by Sekaran influence."

"So, the people could rise up if they're made aware."

Cudree's insectoid arms vibrated. "That's the hope of getting to the communications tower. But I can't guarantee it will work."

It all came back to faith. The Arasu around her seemed so nervous. They were looking to her to guidance, for leadership. For some sort of assurance it was all going to be all right. That's what they were stuck on. She could see it in their body language, even though she could hardly make out any expressions on their alien faces.

But what could she say? She couldn't lie to them and guarantee a success. She had no idea about the specifics of this world, how upset the people were with the Sekarans. It wasn't like Konsin or Deklyn, where she knew the people would be with her. Even then, she'd had Drin's leadership. It was up to her now.

"We'll have to pray for God's blessing," Anais said.

"You mentioned this God before." Cudree shook his head. "I do not know, but it can't hurt to have the blessing of a deity."

"No, it can't," Anais said. "If you'll all quiet..." She had to figure out how to do this. She'd had less experience with overseeing a big group prayer than she did with leading a battle. Her fur stood on edge on the back of her neck, nervousness overcoming her. But she'd brought it up. This was what Drin would have done, so she could do it, too. If anything, it would give some of the Arasu peace in their decisions. She cleared her throat. "Okay, close your eyes, and I'll lead."

It was a stupid statement, as the Arasu didn't seem to have eyelids. Hopefully it communicated the intent of reverence all the same. She closed her eyes and bowed her head. "Dear God...

Yezuah... Please watch over us on this day. We are your creatures, and we need your love and strength to fill us."

In that moment, it was like a great presence surrounded her, held her, made her warm. She could feel the Spirit of God here in the room with her. It gave her more confidence. "Help us to do your will, and to keep you in mind as we go into battle. Vanquish your enemies and free these people from their bonds so we might bring glory to you."

Anais opened her eyes again. "Amen," she said.

"Amen," a few of the Arasu muttered around the room. It seemed not all of them were unfamiliar with the concept of prayer.

It might have been her imagination, but the room seemed to be a little less nervous, less tense. The Arasu looked to her as if asking for more, but it was all she could give them. She clapped her hands together. "Okay. Let's all rest up and make sure we're all ready to go. We're going to need to have our best focus if we're going to succeed. Let's kick these Sekarans off this world!"

The surrounding Arasu cheered.

TWENTY-ONE

DRIN AND ERR-DIO EDGED AROUND THE SHEER ROCK WALL OF
the cave until they found the opening where they'd first descended
into the city.

They wound their way back to the fork in the path. Drin
slowed as they approached, in case the Sekarans were present.

He shifted his vision to track heat signatures. He wasn't sure if
they'd work through the walls. If it were thick rock, the nanites
would not be effective, but the hexagonal combs lining the cave
were hollow, which meant he had a chance at spotting some heat
signatures he wouldn't have under normal conditions.

They came to a halt. Drin focused on his vision. Power trans-
ferred into his sensory extensions, the nanites reaching out into the
hollow combs. They extended, and at first, Drin saw nothing, but
soon, in a faint blue-green color, he spotted shapes of bipedal life
forms. They stood guard around the corner.

He turned to Err-dio, making a hand gesture to him like
pulling a trigger. If Err-dio had spent more time training with him
and the Templars, he could have learned some of the hand

gestures Drin and his brothers used to communicate in stealth battle situations.

Err-dio appeared to understand. He motioned with his laser-repeater, appearing to understand the battle would be coming soon.

Drin formed a light sword in his hand. It glowed in the dark cave. He considered waiting to form his weapon until he was in sight of the enemy, but it would be better to move into action without waiting. The enemy couldn't see them for now, and they would be surprised, even if they were here to guard the entrance to the superweapon's chamber.

Drin and Err-dio moved forward and stopped again just before a bend in the pathway. Drin looked back to Err-dio one more time to confirm. The Skree nodded. *Power and glory to Yezuah*, Drin mouthed to himself.

With all of his speed and strength, Drin took off running, his light sword ahead of him. He made no battle cry, trying to keep quiet, though his footsteps crunched on the ground as rocks crumbled beneath his feet.

The corridor was small. The Sekaran enemy stood in twos, six of them in total. Drin did all he could to ram through them, cutting through enemy flesh with ease. Unfortunately, too many of them clustered together. Drin managed to get through the first two and cut into the gut of one of the second line. The second Sekaran kicked Drin hard, stopping his momentum and forcing him into a side wall.

Err-dio advanced right behind Drin, shooting the Sekaran who kicked Drin, causing the enemy to stumble backward.

The third line had already backed further into the corridor, firing their laser-repeaters toward Drin and Err-dio with reckless abandon. Several of their shots hit the cave walls on the sides, causing the formations to crumble and collapse and debris to fly within the corridor.

Drin positioned himself to absorb the blasts so Err-dio wouldn't be at risk. His shields could extend through most of this corridor.

The Sekarans pelted him with their laser-repeaters. Each step forward was met with resistance, and the Sekarans kept retreating through the corridor the opposite way. Drin needed to push forward and catch up with them before they whittled away his defenses.

He burst into a run again, but the Sekarans were wise to his move this time, ducking under his blade. One tripped him, causing Drin to fall forward and past their line. It left Err-dio exposed on the other side.

Drin smashed into the hard ground, his nanite armor absorbing most of the hit. He pushed himself to his feet immediately, reforming the light sword that dissipated during the fall.

He turned to find both of the Sekarans had fallen along with him. They weren't moving. Err-dio stood over them, holding his smoking laser-repeater. "I've gotten more accurate," Err-dio said.

"Well done," Drin said.

The words seemed to please Err-dio, whose face broke into a wide grin. "Not too bad," he said.

"We haven't gotten to the open cave yet. There were dozens of them in there," Drin said.

They continued down the path toward the wide opening. No more Sekarans met them during their walk, which made Drin uneasy. If the enemy knew they were there, why were they so quiet? They should have had a full complement here to deal with him.

A small light came from the opening beyond, reflecting onto the stalactites on the ceiling. Drin made his way out to the ledge where he'd overlooked and seen the machine before. Where he'd seen the giant rings rotating around a device, there was nothing but dirt now. The cave below was empty.

"This isn't good," Err-dio said.

"No," Drin agreed. "I'm going to jump down below."

Err-dio glanced around. "There's a small trail down, it wraps around the corridor. See it?" He pointed to it. "I'll meet you down there."

Drin nodded. He stepped to the end of the ledge and leaped.

The wind beat against his visor as he descended into the depths of the cavern. Finally, he hit the ground, bending his knees to maintain his balance and absorb the shock. The nanites did most of the work, and the landing was easy, kicking up dust from beneath his boots.

Now that he was closer, he could see tread marks where the Sekarans had moved the device. It led toward a different corridor, a much thicker one designed for vehicles to enter and exit. He moved toward the corridor, but as he did, a full Sekaran unit stepped out of the shadows.

There were at least twenty of them, laser-repeaters drawn. Two of them had physical light swords. None appeared to be holding any EMP devices—grenades that had knocked out his nanites in the past. One small thing to be grateful for. Even with his nanites, their numbers would be overwhelming.

He wanted to call out to Err-dio, for his companion to retreat, but didn't want to draw attention to him.

"Eltu will triumph, infidel!" One of the Sekarans shouted.

Drin gritted his teeth. "You'll be meeting your prophet soon enough."

The laser fire came, lighting up the cavern in brilliant colors. Drin went into a slide, ducking under most of it and causing some of the Sekarans to hit each other with friendly fire. His momentum carried him toward two of the soldiers, and he swung his light sword around, cutting the legs off his targets.

They howled in pain, creating a greater distraction. He used the upper body of one he'd just cut as a shield against some of the incoming fire, letting the Sekarans pelt their companion over and over, before throwing him aside and turning to face an enemy next to him.

This Sekaran had a light sword, driving the hilt down toward Drin's arm. Drin raised his blade, managing to block the energy with his own, narrowly avoiding having his arm sliced off.

Drin parried with the Sekaran twice and dodged a third strike by his aggressive enemy. It left his back to the other Sekarans, who took advantage of the opportunity by firing directly at him.

His shielding flickered, taking too many hits from too many sources. He'd made a mistake in engaging this Sekaran, but there was nothing he could do about it now. His dueling enemy was strong and fast, and Drin wouldn't last very long at this rate.

The two energy blades clashed in the air again, sparking and illuminating their small section of the cavern. The dust picked up, which would be to Drin's advantage, making it harder for the shooters to spot him.

Several laser bolts fired past him—not at him. The shots targeted the area behind him. Drin couldn't afford to look back, but he heard cries of pain and muffled gurgles of men dying. Eyeing past his immediate opponent, Drin spotted Err-dio, who'd descended and now engaged in the battle.

"Stay back!" Drin shouted.

Confusion crossed his opponent's face, and for the first time since they'd engaged, Drin spotted an opening.

He drove his light sword straight forward, toward the Sekaran's belly. The sword-wielder dodged to the side, but wasn't fast enough. Drin clipped his side, opening a wound. Flesh sizzled and burned, and the Sekaran gritted his teeth.

"You're going to pay for that, Elorian," the Sekaran said.

Drin's enemy advanced, his movements turning into heavy hacks of his sword. His strength and momentum was enough to drive Drin backward, out of the hazy dust, and into the view of the other Sekarans.

Despite Err-dio's best efforts, bolts pelted Drin, one getting through his shielding and hitting him in the calf. The pain reverberated through Drin like a tidal wave, and he growled to release some of it. The sound echoed into the cavern.

He couldn't stay on his feet, and dropped to his knees. The Sekaran sword-wielder looked pleased with the situation, bringing his blade upward, grasping the hilt with both hands while pointing the energy at Drin's face.

In a desperate effort to survive, Drin released his light sword, flinging it so it spun toward the Sekaran. It was a risky move, but had he not acted in the moment, he would have faced certain death. His blade found his opponent's legs, slicing through them as if the Sekaran wore no armor. It was one of the benefits of a light sword. The energy was so intense it could pierce most objects.

The Sekaran's jaw went slack, confused by his sudden lack of legs. Shock crossed his face, and his eyes went wide. Disconnected, his legs could no longer support his upper body weight. They fell, and the torso of the Sekaran slid to the side. The swordsman tried one last desperate effort to swing his blade.

Drin rolled in the opposite direction of the Sekaran's fall. The Sekaran's blade hit dirt, missing Drin entirely.

With a mental command, Drin dissipated his light sword and reformed it in his hand. He pushed himself up on his good leg, lunging forward and striking hard at the Sekaran's chest. Off balance and helpless, the Sekaran could do little but convulse and die. He had been a worthy opponent.

Drin couldn't keep his balance after the momentum of his push. His leg still stung too badly from being blasted. He couldn't stand, falling face-first to the ground.

Err-dio jumped forward, helping Drin up with one arm, while

still laying down suppression fire with his laser-repeater in his other hand. He wouldn't be accurate that way, but it didn't matter.

"I told you to stay back," Drin said.

"My apologies, Templar. I will do penance later," Err-dio said.

"Are you being flippant?" Drin asked, narrowing his eyes.

Before Err-dio could respond, laser bolts zoomed in their direction. Drin turned to position himself in front of the Skree, allowing his shields to absorb the blasts.

Err-dio straightened and fired toward the targets. He struck one Sekaran, and then another.

"The Elorian has back-up. Retreat and form up with the others!" one Sekaran shouted.

The blasts stopped coming as the remaining Sekarans ran down the tunnel where the tracks led. There would be a lot more Sekarans to deal with later.

"Thankfully, there wasn't a battlemage in this group," Err-dio said.

"If there had been, we wouldn't have survived," Drin said. "These soldiers are better trained than ones I've faced in the past. I wonder who their warlord is."

Err-dio guided Drin over to a rock where he could sit and rest. "I suppose we'll find out in time. How long will your wound take to heal?" He cocked his head to get a view of Drin's calf.

Blood had dried on it, cauterized by his nanites. Drin stretched his foot, finding the pain to be excruciating. A minute prior, he wouldn't have been able to move it at all, however.

"Cover the entrance in case they come back," Drin said.

Err-dio stepped toward the larger corridor, leveling his laser-repeater at the opening.

It wasn't the ideal back-up. He'd much rather have a contingent of Templars with him for such a crucial mission, but Err-dio had strong faith. They would fight together.

Drin closed his eyes, immediately falling into his breathing exercises. The low amount of movement and meditation helped the nanites to heal him, to recover themselves as they prepared for the next engagement. He lost himself in the darkness, in the wholeness of the spirit of God. *Praise Yezuah for all the blessings you've bestowed upon me.*

Despite clearing his mind, images flashed in his head. A pulsing light in the darkness. It was difficult to make out what it was, but it seemed to be nearby. It was calling to him.

Lord? Drin asked silently.

No response.

Time passed, no real way to tell how much. It must have been at least an hour. Drin opened his eyes again and saw Err-dio standing in the same position, faithfully fixed upon the corridor opening.

Drin pushed himself to his feet. His calf was still sore, but he could put weight on it. The nanites were truly miraculous. A blessing from God. It was a good reminder to focus on the divine tasks at hand. "My healing's complete," Drin said.

Err-dio jumped, spinning to see him. He laughed. "I wasn't expecting you to speak. I was very focused."

"You did well," Drin said.

"I didn't have to do much."

"We need to find out where the Sekarans are going with the superweapon." Drin glanced around the cavern floor. One of the Sekarans stirred, or rather writhed in pain on the ground. He was lucky Err-dio hadn't put the infidel out of his misery.

He motioned to Err-dio to follow and crouched by the Sekaran, flipping the man onto his back. He had a terrible wound. Drin formed his light sword in his hand and placed it up against the Sekaran's throat, careful not to touch the skin, but keeping it close enough the Sekaran felt the heat from it. "I want to know where the superweapon is headed," Drin said.

The Sekaran seemed as if he barely understood where he was. "It's gone. Requisitioned."

"To where?"

"A dreadnought in orbit... It's going to be deployed..."

"Where?"

The Sekaran stopped breathing. Drin had been lucky to get this much out of him. Drin released the man's shirt and let him fall back to the ground.

"What now?" Err-dio asked.

Drin pushed himself to his feet, letting his light sword dissipate. "We need to get to the surface and find a way to stop the Sekarans from reaching their capital ship."

"I'll pray the Lord's blessing on us."

Drin stepped toward the winding path Err-dio had just taken to get down here. "Good. We're going to need it."

"We're not going to take the path to follow the Sekarans out?"

"No, they'll be waiting for us. We should go back up to the city above and see if we can cut them off as they leave."

They began the long hike up the cave wall together.

TWENTY-TWO

The Arasu outfitted Anais with an earpiece comm unit. It was designed for Arasu, so they had to figure out a way to wrap a band around Anais' flopping ears for it to stay, but they managed to make it work. She entered into the strange rock city with three Arasu, including Fardree. The Arasu had laser-repeaters. One was offered to Anais, but she didn't need one. She could create armor and a light sword at will, and she needed more practice with the Templar weapon.

She stepped to the side to allow the rest of the Arasu resistance a way out of their makeshift hideaway. Far more of the bug creatures came flooding outward than she had realized were inside the cave to begin with. Hundreds of them entered the streets, and they spread out in all directions. Chaos.

She had a clear direction to go—toward the cave where the Sekarans made their base. She was up to the task.

The fighting started. Anais could hear the sound of vehicles stopping, laser-repeaters firing, and people yelling at each other. It was coming from the opposite direction, and she was glad she didn't have to enter into the conflict.

"We've encountered the police," Cudree said through her earpiece. "They've not dispatched their riot teams yet, only standard law enforcement. The first two cars have been contained."

Anais picked up her pace, not wanting to get caught in the greater conflict. Once Cudree seized the communication control tower, things were going to get even crazier.

Her team stayed by her, pointing their weapons in different directions at every sound. They were jumpy, but she couldn't blame them. If she'd never been in a conflict like this before, she would be, as well. But she had been, and a calm flowed through her she hadn't experienced in the prior battles. Was this what experience was supposed to feel like?

Before she could answer the question, a new experience overcame her in the form of a circular shadow descending over her head.

She looked up.

Descending from the higher reaches of the cavern, blocking the light of the street lamps, was a hovering circle. It blew the air from under it, causing wind to flow into Anais' face. Her armor stopped the bulk of it but she could feel the warm air.

As the hovering circle descended, Anais saw three armored personnel on it. They had to have been the local police.

Her companions opened fire, the bolts hitting a transparent shield on the hover-chariot. The police fired back, shooting one of her Arasu companions. The other two ran behind parked vehicles to take cover.

Anais formed her light sword and stepped forward, not fearing these police. They didn't know what they were dealing with. In some ways, she had sympathy for them, but she didn't have time to get slowed down by these people. She stepped through the shield, forcing the Arasu police off the chariot, backing away from her.

They fired their laser-repeaters, bolts blasting against her nanite shielding. Though they wore darkened visors, Anais could sense the fear in them.

She hurdled over the chariot, moving forward within a blur of motion. In one slice of her blade, she managed to fell two of the police. The third stumbled backward, still firing at her to no avail.

Her companions blasted him with their laser-repeaters. He took several shots, spinning uncontrollably from the force of the blasts before hitting the pavement.

"Let's go!" Anais shouted, motioning with her light sword, then pressing forward. Timing was crucial, she understood that from the frantic way Cudree led his people. If the Sekarans managed to get out of their cave and flood the streets, this revolt might be over as quickly as it began.

The three remaining of Anais's team moved to the cavern's edge and crept around the rock face. It was a good position because it would prevent them from being ambushed—they could see enemies coming.

"We've reached the communications tower," Cudree said through the earpiece. "Sensors here are showing the Sekarans are gathering at the northern landing pad in Horiz Canyon. It appears as if they're preparing a ship for launch."

Would the Sekarans be folding so easily? Anais didn't think so. It was an odd report, nonetheless. As they approached the cave entrance, she'd expected to see Sekaran troops rushing through to deal with the riot, but there were none in sight. As much as it boded well for her immediate mission, it didn't feel right.

Cudree's voice came over the city loudspeakers. "Greetings fellow Arasu. You should know our world has been betrayed. Our leaders have been in talks with the Sekarans, who did not leave our planet as we had originally thought. They've been underground, working, using us. Minister Zebee has sold us out to the Sekarans. Their plan is to make us economically dependent on their schemes so we are forced into indentured servitude in the future."

Mutters rose from the center of town. Cries, yells in agreement, along with others who sounded angry. Anais couldn't tell what the result of Cudree's message would be. She hoped he had enough support.

"I urge all of you, fellow citizens—rise up! Join in our fight against our oppressors. Help us take the government buildings. Help us to secure the caves where the Sekarans have been hiding. Help us to purge them from our lands. There will be leaders in the streets. We'll be easy to find. We will move forward together, for a new Arasu, a free Arasu!"

More cheers came.

Anais reached the cave opening a moment later. There was a big step up to a metal door that was open, leading to a small passageway into darkness. It was very similar to the hideaway where she'd met with the Arasu resistance. How many small fissures and hidden caves were there in this city? On this planet? It had to make for a lot of secrecy with these people.

Fardree pressed one his stalk-like arms to the cave wall. "We need to get some kind of explosive charges to blow this entrance," he said. "I don't think laser-repeaters will do enough damage to close it off quickly."

"No need," Anais said. She formed a light sword in her hand. "I can cut through the majority of the rock." She looked upward. "And I can leap to the top to make the rocks cave in. Give me space."

The two Arasu backed away from her, allowing her to do her work with her sword.

Anais bent her knees, preparing to leap, when shadows moved from within the cave. "They're coming!" she said.

The Arasu leveled their laser-repeaters at the entrance. Anais stood ready to fight. She wasn't sure if it was a good idea to leap and expose herself with the enemies so close, so she held her position, spreading her legs into a comfortable stance like Drin had taught her.

Through the entrance came a surprise. It wasn't Sekarans like she had expected—a Skree came through the aperture, holding onto a laser-repeater. The Arasu didn't seem to differentiate. They fired.

"Wait!" Anais shouted. "Hold your fire!"

The blasts narrowly missed Err-dio, who held his weapon up. Behind him was a man standing in similar gray armor to Anais—Elorian armor. It had to be Drin.

Her shout had been enough to influence Err-dio, who recoiled in surprise, but didn't return fire against the Arasu. He cocked his head toward Anais, surprise on his face. Then, he jumped down to stand in front of her. "Anais?"

"What are you doing here?" she asked.

"I could ask you the same thing!"

Drin hopped down after Err-dio. As he did, he let his light sword dissipate into the air, same with his helmet, revealing his green-skinned Elorian features. His thin lips were pressed tightly together, eyes surveying with as deep a seriousness as ever.

No smiles for her, but did she expect it of him? Anais didn't care. She dissipated her light sword and pushed past Err-dio to fling her arms around Drin's neck. "Drin! I'm so glad to see you." Despite herself, tears formed in her eyes. She wished she could control her emotions better, but she was just so happy to see him, she didn't care.

"Likewise," Drin said, tepidly patting her sides. He pulled back from her embrace. "I, too, am interested as to what you're doing here. However, this is a very dangerous place right now."

"I know it is," Anais said, glancing back over her shoulder. The Arasu were still standing there with guns raised. She couldn't read their expressions, but they had to be confused. "It's okay. These are friends," she said.

"Will they be helping us to seal the cave?" Fardree asked.

"I would advise against it. I'm going to need to get back into the cave once we've finished our current mission," Drin said.

"But our orders—"

"If Drin says we need to do something, we should do it," Anais said. "You remember the stories I told you about the Elorians when I was in your hideaway?"

Fardree nodded.

"He's the one who liberated my world," Anais said.

"And mine as well," Err-dio said.

"Trust him. He'll do the same for your world if you let him," Anais said.

Drin inclined his head. He didn't say anything, but Anais could sense his pride. Their nanites must have been interacting again. It felt good. His had some damage to them, and hers naturally moved to heal his. Though it drained some energy from her, it instilled her with a sense of purpose. She loved supporting Drin because she loved him.

"We'll have to swap stories later," Drin said. "Right now, the Sekarans are planning to leave for orbit, and we have to put a stop to them. We need to get to your spaceport, or whatever your equivalent of one is."

"I just heard over the comm that the Sekarans were getting ready to depart from a place called Horiz Canyon," Anais said.

"I know where that is. I can lead you," Fardree said.

"Then let's go," Drin said.

TWENTY-THREE

Drin's party hurried through the streets. Fighting erupted everywhere, a full civil war between the police and Sekaran loyalists against insurgents who were fed up with Sekaran rule. It was impossible to tell who was who or which side was winning. The Arasu didn't look all that different from one another, but it didn't matter for what Drin needed to accomplish.

He needed to stop the Sekarans. If they managed to get the superweapon off this world, the entire galaxy could be at risk. It made this minor civil war seem meaningless in comparison.

Anais's friend led them into the city. Drin tried to look menacing in his armor with his light sword drawn to deter anyone from trying to involve them in their conflict. They couldn't spare any time.

As he had the thought, a high-pitched sound pierced his skull. Blinding light overcame him. It washed in front of his eyes, everything in the world fading in front of him. His body went weak, his knees buckling and causing him to fall to the ground. He managed to brace himself with his hands, but it felt like someone drove a spike through the back of his skull, making it impossible for him to raise his head.

Your path is in the cave.

The thought popped into his head. But it wasn't his. Anais? Was she connecting with him with her nanites?

No, this didn't have her voice, or her tender concern. Whatever spoke to him felt much bigger, more ominous.

"God?" Drin asked.

Nothing responded to him.

His vision slowly restored. The light faded from him, and the smooth surface of the streets appeared before his eyes. His hands held him up off the ground, but they shook. Drin leaned back on his knees.

Both Anais and Err-dio had knelt beside him, each taking an arm. Worry was plastered on their faces.

"Are you all right, Drin?" Anais asked. "What happened?"

"Do you think it's a problem with the nanites? Have you overexerted yourself?" Err-dio asked.

The truth was, Drin had no idea what had just occurred. It could very well be the nanites. His rests and respites had been brief, but this had been a fairly easy battlefront compared to Konsin II or Deklyn. Those he had fought much harder before his nanites gave way. Perhaps it was the accumulation of all the fighting he'd done in recent months? Could he have put too much strain on his system?

He had no way of knowing, and without someone from the church—who understood the nanites—to medically diagnose him, all he would have would be conjecture. It did no good. "No, I think my nanites are functioning normally. My visor states they're at eighty-five percent efficiency."

"You're not telling us everything," Anais said.

The girl could read far too much into him ever since her nanite field merged with his. It was impossible to keep anything to himself, which made it even harder to protect her. It irritated Drin. "No, I'm not."

A small explosion rumbled deeper in the city.

Anais glanced over her shoulder. "We have to get going, as you said. I don't think we have much time."

Drin pushed himself to his feet. Err-dio and Anais helped him to right himself. He had fully recovered and had no problems with his balance. But he'd had a vision. It was a strange one, much like the apostles had in the Holy Book after Yezuah ascended into heaven. He couldn't discount that God may have been speaking to him directly. His instincts told him to follow the command he'd received. "You'll have to go without me."

"What?" Anais asked, her helmet disappearing to reveal concern in her face. "We shouldn't separate again."

"My path lies back in the cave we just left. I've escorted you this far. I believe you'll be fine," Drin said.

"But the Sekarans..."

Drin placed his hands on her arms, squeezing her softly. "You can do it. Have faith. You lead just as well as I can. You have the tools—both the nanites and everything I've taught you."

Anais bit her lip, not looking like she was convinced. "This is all very strange."

"I know," Drin said. "I'll tell you of it later. You have to stop them. Have faith and it will be so."

The girl pulled him in for a tight hug, pressing her face against his chest. It was her way of saying goodbye, where she could show him affection. It filled him with warmth.

Drin cautiously wrapped his arms around her and squeezed again.

"Let's go," Err-dio said. "We will perform our duty faithfully, Templar."

"Thank you," Drin said, pulling back from Anais. His friend didn't question him, even after the strange incident that must have looked like a seizure from the outside. It was true trust. Love. The brotherly kind, just as Yezuah had promised and commanded to his followers. Drin was proud of his friends.

Silence hung in the air, as no one wanted to split up again. But it must be so. Drin had to find out if this truly was a call from the Lord for him to go deeper into the cavern. It had to have been.

It was a whisper before in the cave, and shaking him to his senses now. He didn't dare avoid the call a third time. He'd read enough stories in the Holy Book of what happened to reluctant prophets when they didn't heed the call even then.

The others nodded and departed, rushing toward the basin beyond the city. Drin turned and strode back toward the cavern. He ignored the fighting around him. The Arasu civil war didn't concern him, only God's will.

TWENTY-FOUR

ANAIS AND HER GROUP REACHED THE LANDING AREA IN Horiz Canyon. The makeshift spaceport was carved out of the rock, just above the lower floor. Steps spiraled up to the pad, where a dozen ships were parked. A control tower was embedded in the rocks above, with a giant glass face looking down upon the pad. Several Arasu stood in the tower, with holographic displays in front of them, translucent so the controllers could see the ships they directed.

A transport lifted off the ground, its thrusters firing, pushing the ship into the air. A billowy cloud of dust grew on the platform. The Arasu averted their eyes, but Anais had her helmet and visor formed, so she could watch the shuttle go. Was this the Sekaran vessel they were supposed to hunt down? She had a feeling it was. "We have to hurry. I think they just took off," Anais said.

She rushed up the stairs on the side of the landing pad. At the top were several Arasu and a small contingent of Sekarans. They seemed to recognize her Elorian armor as they raised weapons and took up defensive positions. Anais took a deep breath and willed a light sword into existence. It was a strange sensation still, being able to do this, but she grew more confident in her abilities each time she created a weapon with her nanites.

Laser bolts came flying at her.

"Stay in cover!" Anais said. She had this. She could absorb some of the hits. The others, not so much.

She pressed forward toward the Sekarans. Bolts pelted into her shielding. She waved her blade around, trying to mimic the way Drin could flip his and intimidate his enemies. Her skill with the blade wasn't nearly in the realm of his, but she thought she put on a decent show with it.

As the Sekarans saw their laser fire had little effect, they began retreating.

Anais had to press her advantage. She jumped forward. Her nanites took over and allowed her to bound over one of the shuttles. She flew right past a Sekaran, sliding her boots on the pavement to force herself to a stop. Then, she spun and swung her light sword hard into the Sekaran's torso.

It cut right through the soldier, and he fell to the ground, dropping his weapon.

"I did it," Anais said. The move reminded her of Drin. He would have been proud.

He had acted so strange merely minutes before. She'd learned not to question his methods. Sometimes everything he did seemed to make no sense, but it had worked out every time so far. Worry knotted her stomach.

There were four other Sekarans mixed in with the Arasu, and they ran for the cover of a door in the rock face, firing back along the way. Anais didn't follow. She wasn't here to keep a battle going.

Instead, she turned to look for her companions. They had ascended the ramp, carefully staying out of the firefight and using one of the other shuttles as cover. Anais stepped around one side, and Err-dio peeked his head from around it.

"Are we clear?" Err-dio asked.

"For now," Anais said.

The Sekarans had barred the door where they hid. Anais moved to her friends.

Err-dio nodded. "Good." He motioned to the shuttle the others hid behind. "This shuttle is the same type as the one that just took off. Perhaps we can use it?"

"How are we going to get it to operate?"

Err-dio grinned. "I have ways. I used to have to hijack all kinds of Sekaran ships on Altequine." He turned and popped open a panel, which displayed several wires and a small screen with some buttons. He went to work on it, and a ramp dropped from the side of the shuttle. The bottom of the ramp clanged against the platform. "Hop in," Err-dio said.

The Arasu made their way into the shuttle, and Anais joined them. Err-dio popped the panel back into place and then made his way inside. He scooted past the others to the front of the craft where he crouched and pulled wires out from underneath the piloting console. "I'll need to bypass the command codes to get this lifted. Should take me just a second. If you wouldn't mind closing the ramp? It's the button up on the wall on the right, by where it lowered."

Anais spotted the button and hit it. The ramp lifted and sealed the shuttle a moment later.

Laser fire came from outside, rocking the shuttle. The Sekarans must have spotted her leaving and saw the danger was clear. "I think we should hurry this up if we don't want to get blown to bits in here," Anais said.

"I'm going as fast as I can," Err-dio said.

Fardree and the other Arasu glanced at each other but didn't seem to have anything to add to the conversation.

Anais fell back into one of the seats in the rear of the craft, unable to do anything else but wait.

"Got it," Err-dio said before sliding into the pilot's chair. He tapped controls and flipped switches above him.

More laser fire hit the craft, rumbling when it connected.

"I hope it's not hitting anything important," Fardree said.

"Me too," Err-dio said. The engines powered up. Err-dio slid his fingers up along the thrusters' power track, and the rumbling grew. The ship blasted off, another dust cloud pluming underneath them. More laser shots hit the bottom of the ship, but they didn't seem to pierce the hull.

The shuttle shot up into the clouds. The sensation caused her stomach to feel like it lifted into her throat for a moment. Even though she didn't get space-sick like some of her people when they lifted out of an atmosphere, she gasped. "Err-dio!"

"Sorry. I didn't think it'd be a good idea to take more fire. Who knows what could have happened? I decided to get us out of range as fast as possible," Err-dio said, adjusting the controls as he shifted the craft's trajectory.

"A little warning would be nice, next time," Anais said.

Fardree moved to the co-piloting station, pulling up sensor display. "The craft ahead of us isn't too far ahead. They didn't rush up into the sky like we did." He pointed to a blip on the map. "Here."

"Excellent," Err-dio said, tapping more controls. "I've set the ship's AI to follow the other craft. Wherever she's going, we'll follow."

They broke out of the atmosphere and into space. The sky darkened, the atmosphere dissipating into a small blue aura behind them. Stars filled the view from up front.

Several other blips appeared on Fardree's screen. The display made a chirping noise.

"What's that?" Anais asked.

Fardree zoomed in on the display, calling up a view of the

ships further ahead, which were still too far off to see through a natural view. "Oh no," he said.

Err-dio leaned over to take a look. "Hmm?"

"What is it?" Anais asked.

"There's a Sekaran warship ahead. It looks like our target is headed directly for it. The ship is flanked by several other Sekaran ships."

This wasn't good at all. Their enemies had reinforcements—and that shuttle had a weapon on it with the potential to destroy worlds. What if they spotted her ship?

Anais realized she'd been holding her breath and exhaled. She didn't know what to do. She didn't have the power to fight a Sekaran ship, did she? Not in this shuttle.

She watched Fardree's display. The other shuttle maneuvered into a landing position, making its entrance into the Sekaran battleship's docking bay. Its thrusters fired for a slow descent, and the shuttle was soon enveloped by the hulking monstrosity of a ship.

"What do we do?" Err-dio asked, looking back at her.

The others all stared at her. They wanted her guidance. But she was no battle leader, despite Drin giving her reassurances. Her ears twitched. They couldn't fight the Sekaran battleship head-on. But they also couldn't just leave or head back to the planet. They needed to take care of this superweapon. For Drin, for the Arasu people, and anyone else who might come under its path of fire.

"We act like we're another load of Sekaran soldiers and dock with them. Do you think you can pull it off?" Anais asked.

Err-dio tapped some commands. "I see the communications channel from the first shuttle to the Sekarans from a few minutes ago. They sent their codes without encryption. Let me try to send the same codes and see what happens." He input the codes into the communications console.

They waited. It felt like an eternity passed before the Sekarans responded, but then the comm console chirped.

"Is that good?" Anais asked.

"They're allowing us to dock," Err-dio said. He didn't sound like he was so sure it was a good thing.

He adjusted their coordinates and prepared the shuttle for landing. The AI took over, bringing them in slowly, just like the vessel before them. The Sekaran ship grew in front of them until it encompassed their entire view. Soon, they could see the shuttle bay, a wide opening, square, where a forcefield dropped to allow them entry.

The interior of the shuttle bay shone a metallic color, the images of the docked shuttles hazily reflected on its surface. The other shuttle was in the center of the room, and docking crews worked with respirators and in-flight suits so they wouldn't have issues with decompression and vacuum.

Guards waited behind another forcefield, at least twenty Sekarans in full armor with laser-repeater rifles. This was a terrible idea. Dread filled her, causing her shoulders to tense and her head to feel light. She had to concentrate and focus. Just like Drin taught her, she tried breathing exercises. In through the nose, out through the mouth. Slowly. It didn't seem to have any effect in calming her.

The ship landed. The AI set them down softly, but with a small jolt. The other shuttle was in clear view. The shuttle bay repressurized, and a ramp descended from the Sekaran transport.

A group of four Sekarans, using magnetic lifters to haul the giant device, descended the ramp. The superweapon levitated off the ground, casting a shadow beneath it. It didn't appear to be powered up. As it was, it didn't seem dangerous at all, just a hunk of metal being carried by four soldiers.

Err-dio moved to the back of the craft. "We should be careful about letting them see anyone but Arasu for the time being. We'll need every edge we can get," he said.

Fardree followed Err-dio back soon afterward. "You're not thinking of trying to fight in *here?*"

"I don't see any other choice," Anais said. She stood, clenching a little lip in her armor just at her waist. It was the only thing she could grab onto, and she needed something to hold. The truth was, she had just as bad a feeling about this as Fardree did. They had very little shot at coming out of this shuttle bay alive.

But at least they could destroy that deadly weapon and save billions of lives.

Sometimes, one had to sacrifice for the greater good.

The thought comforted her. It would have made Drin proud if he could have heard her say those words. She wished she could have seen him one last time. All of their moments together flashed before her eyes. His rescue of her from the stoning pit of Altequine. Him rescuing her again from a Sekaran warlord. His saving her life. Her returning the favor. Their time together on Deklyn, especially those moments training together. It tugged at her heart to think those might have been her last moments to be with him. But at least they were good times. At least there was love.

Anais nodded to herself to firm her resolve. "Okay. Let's take out that weapon."

TWENTY-FIVE

Drin wound his way back into the big cavern, where the Sekarans had dug out their superweapon. It seemed so empty now. Quiet. Still. Dark. In some ways it was peaceful, but it also gave him an uneasy feeling. The cavern was devoid of life. The air was stagnant, unmoving, unchanging. This was what hell must have been life, separation from God, and everything else, with no way out.

He had a way out. He could still turn back, couldn't he? Why was he so nervous about this? God had given him a vision. His task was clear. He couldn't shake the dread growing inside of him, as irrational as it might have been.

And it was irrational. He had the nanites, Yezuah's gift unto the Elorian Templars. How did the verse go? *Even in the darkest depths, you will stand by me and guide me.* God had made that promise to his faithful.

Drin stopped his descent into the cave. He dropped to his knees and folded his hands. No one was around. He could afford the time and the gesture. He had to humble himself before the Lord. It always proved to be the right path.

Dear Lord, Drin prayed silently, *help me to follow your will. Forgive my sins and all of my fleshly desires. Keep me pure so I might be a light to this world in your name. All glory and power to you, Lord Yezuah.*

"Amen," Drin said aloud.

He pushed himself back to his feet and continued into the cave. The place where the superweapon had been was indented, like a small crater into the ground. The device must have been very heavy. But there was another corridor behind it, leading to even greater depths. Drin entered the deeper corridor.

No lights lay ahead, but it didn't matter for Drin. He switched on his night vision.

It didn't work.

Drin tensed his forehead, trying to will his nanites into his desired function. Still nothing. He tried to form a light sword, but again, he found himself unable to create any light.

This was disconcerting. No light. There was definitely something foul with this cavern. He could feel it all around him like immense pressure trying to close in on him. But he wouldn't be afraid. The Lord was with him. He would be Drin's guide.

Drin pushed further into the cavern, using his hands to feel along the jagged edges of the rock to find his way through. It was tight in some spots but seemed to open more in further. He had to move slowly because of the lack of light. He nearly tripped over protruding rocks from the floor more than a few times.

The winding cavern seemed to go on forever and then opened into a large room again. With the pitch blackness, it was impossible to tell how big the room was. Drin didn't dare move from his place beside the wall, lest he get lost in here forever. This was strange indeed. How far into the depths of this world had he gone?

The sound of dripping water echoed in the chamber. The drips came slowly, but there must have been some sort of water table here. Was it what rose into the city above to create the flooding?

As if in answer to his question, the dripping sound erupted into rushing water. Drin tried to find a ledge to grip himself, as he was fairly certain what was coming. He hoped he could survive it.

The rushing sound intensified. Soon the water hit him as hard as it had the last time. Drin dug his fingers into the rock as best he could, but he wasn't able to keep hold. The force of the water pushed him back into the room, slamming him against the back wall.

Even through the armor, his body jolted. Pain traveled up through the nerves in his back and to his neck. Drin clenched his teeth.

The water still flowed around him, but at least he was at a point where he couldn't be pushed any further. The nanites kept the water out of the suit, and Drin had enough air to survive for several minutes.

The water continued. It must not have been able to reach the raised area of the cave. Otherwise it would have been damp, much like the city streets. The current onslaught of current kept pushing at him, forcing Drin against the wall. He couldn't move.

Time passed, draining his nanites of energy, but fortunately, he had not already depleted them from battle. He was able to maintain consciousness as the water ceased its ascent, and then slowly drained from the cavern.

Drin decided to let the current take him forward, the water carrying him through the room and into yet another corridor. He surfed down rapids, keeping pace with the water, despite being unable to see anything.

Eventually, the water took him to a much larger opening, where Drin resurfaced. A soft illumination came from a domed ceiling, a blue light, which colored everything.

The cavern was enormous, larger than the entire Arasu city

above. Something moved—an avian life form. Whether a rodent or a bird, Drin couldn't tell, but several of them flapped wings in the high ceiling. They had long talons protruding, as well as what appeared to be a sharp beak or jaw. There was also foliage—a moss-like substance, as well as several thin trees, which bore no leaves, but the moss grew up their trunks, as well. The blue light must have acted as a sun to provide the vital nutrients for photo-synthesis. Interesting.

Drin swam to the bank of his river, setting a hand forward first to see if it was solid ground in front of him. It was covered in moss, a cushion, but it appeared solid enough. He pulled himself onto the bank, allowing the nanites to dry his exterior armor.

He attempted to form a light sword again. This time, the blade appeared in his hands. There must have been some sort of damp-ening field within the corridors which didn't allow his nanites to shift. He'd been lucky he'd had armor formed before delving into the place. Otherwise, the rising water would have surely killed him.

There appeared to be several pieces of equipment ahead of him, giant metallic objects with flashing lights. Drin stepped toward them to try to get a closer look.

One of the devices had several man-sized cylinders, which were covered in dust and moss. Vapor wafted from the cylinders, and it made a sound as if a machine were pumping something into it. They were very strange looking.

Drin's presence seemed to activate something. The two cylin-ders opened, their tops popping upward. Vapor clouds poured out over the lip of it. A bright light flashed, momentarily blinding Drin. He tried to cover his eyes.

The light died down, revealing two bright orange forms of energy. They circled together in a figure-eight form, before sepa-rating and doing a loop around Drin. They looked like fireballs, but fire couldn't pulse and glow the way these did. They seemed to light up the whole area around them.

They settled and took what appeared to be an Elorian form. "Invader, you do not belong here," one said.

"I was sent here by the true God, Yezuah," Drin said.

The beings lost form, like the words ripped energy from them. They dissipated but reformed. "You are sent by Him. You'll be destroyed!"

One of the energy beings shot its entire mass toward Drin, its head flying forward through a column of bright orange.

Drin dodged and ran his light sword into the stream of energy. It sparked as if he were cutting through a train full of metal rushing at him, but the energy being didn't appear to be any worse for the wear.

The other one pelted him in the hip while he fought its companion.

The force hit him harder than the wall of water had minutes prior. It felt like it dislodged his hip from his body. Drin stumbled, trying to right himself. "Lord, give me strength," he said to himself.

The energy beings came at him again. Drin dodged both of them this time but was able to make no attack of his own. They were too fast, and they weren't going to let up. He backed away from their cylindrical modules, but they followed.

On their next pass, they came all too close to hitting him. Drin had to drop into a slide to duck under one of the assaults. He came up on the end and righted himself, turning, and hitting the creature with his light sword once more.

Again, it seemed to have no effect. What could he do? He was going to die here because he would tire soon, and these energy beings didn't seem to be bound by the same physical rules he was.

They came at him for a fourth pass. This time, one pelted into his chest, knocking him over. At least one of his ribs cracked in the process. Drin instinctively drew a heavy breath, which only exacerbated the pain the creature had set upon him. He let out a cry.

"Let your pain be known to your master. We will not be bound again!" the energy being shouted. It seemed to come from all over the cavern as if its voice was disembodied.

Your master? This was all so strange. Drin forced himself up anyway as the creatures circled around some of the trees and came back toward him. Who was his master? God? These creatures hated God.

The thought triggered his memory. Stories from the Holy Book. Yezuah had driven out demons with his mere presence, and they sounded much like these creatures did as they attacked him. They'd hated hearing the name before.

They came at him again. This time, Drin held his ground. "By Yezuah, I command you to leave this realm," Drin said.

It worked. Before they could strike him, they faded, losing form. The creatures passed through him to the other side, but they were still there.

"The Lord Yezuah owns this domain. It is His creation. It does not belong to you. Go back to where you came from!" Drin said firmly.

The energy creatures let out shrieks. They sparked again as if they'd been pelted by the laser sword, but it seemed to be all over their beings. Smoke rose from them, and then the energy flashed again, sending another blinding light into the cavern.

The energy beings faded after that, their last gasp and attempt to hold their cohesion. They disappeared into nothingness, and soon, it was as if they'd never existed in the cavern.

Except for Drin's broken rib. The pain made him wince.

He turned back and saw the machinery. There was a much larger machine behind those pods where the energy beings had been kept and sealed. It was the machine pumping the energy into the cavern. It had a platform, steps leading up to it. The machine stood like a column, several feet above Drin's head. It had controls on it, as well, with a pad, which had lights surrounding it.

Drin felt compelled to go to the pad, to stand there. He didn't know what would result from it, but he knew he had to, and he couldn't delay, even to let the nanites go to work on his ribs. He would have to take all of his pain and suffering and move. He didn't know why, but he was certain there wouldn't be much time left.

Yezuah, I pray this is the right path. It had to be. He'd seen demons, they'd recoiled at Yezuah's name. All he could do was keep his faith and hope it would be enough to overcome whatever challenges he was about to encounter.

TWENTY-SIX

As Anais prepared to depart the shuttle, alarms blared in the bay. She stopped herself. "Are they sounding the alarm for us?" she asked.

The others didn't seem to have a good answer, but Fardree peeked into the cockpit, where he still had his tactical display. "I don't think so. More ships have entered the system. From my readings, it doesn't look like the ships we're seeing in the system."

"Can you get more information?" Anais asked.

He slipped back into his co-piloting chair, tapping controls. Different schematics appeared on his display, though written in the Arasu language. "It says the ships entering the system are Elorian."

The news surprised Anais, though it shouldn't have. Drin was on the planet, after all. He could have summoned his friends.

What did it mean for their current situation, though? Should they try to get out of the shuttle bay? No, the ship could easily take off, or maybe even use the superweapon against the Elorian ships. Anais wasn't sure how the device would work. They still had to disable it, even if there were a battle raging outside, and they risked being caught in the crossfire by staying here. "At least they'll be occupied," Anais said. "I think we have to try to take them by surprise. They still believe we're part of the Sekaran team from the surface."

"They'll know better as soon as we open the door," Err-dio said.

"Which is why we have to be ready to fight directly out of the gate. I have my nanite armor. The rest of you should stay back so you don't risk getting hit," Anais said. It didn't give her the confidence as when Drin launched his plans. His always seemed to have a little more to them, but she could at least be useful to the others and absorb some of the early blows from the Sekarans outside.

She let out a deep breath. "Are we all ready?"

The others nodded.

Anais pressed her hand against the ramp controls, opening the side of the shuttlecraft into the Sekaran bay. The craft hissed as its pressure equalized to the outside.

The Sekarans there were too busy to notice her at first. They prepped some of their fighters in the bay. Maybe she could reach the weapon before they found her?

She had no such luck, as the Sekarans noted her armor before she reached the first group of them. These were just technicians. They didn't have weapons, but they shouted and called over some of the Sekaran soldiers in the bay.

Four men marched over, laser-repeaters already in position. They opened fire on Anais.

The bolts hit her shielding, dissipating into the pink radiant light created by the nanites. They didn't seem to harm her. Anais could handle this.

She trudged forward, even though the persistent laser bolts hitting her created force to push her back. The Sekarans kept backing up as they fired, but she could be faster than them. Using her Deklyn agility, she rushed forward, just as she had before. She held her laser sword to the side. Perhaps her form with the blade wasn't as elegant as Drin, but she could get the job done by her quick footwork.

Doing battle was like a dance in a lot of ways, and she had plenty of experience dancing. Drin told her balance and footwork was far more important than any other aspect of a fight, and it appeared he was right.

She ran directly into the line of four Sekarans, slicing through a first just by holding her blade to the side. The soldiers couldn't adjust to her speed fast enough to hit her with any accuracy, especially at this close of range. Anais whirled, felling a second soldier before jabbing her light blade into the gut of a third. One remained, and he backpedaled, maneuvering behind one of the Sekaran troop transports.

Anais followed, glancing back over her shoulder. Err-dio and the two Arasu made their way down the ramp, weapons in hand, being careful. They kept by the shuttle, using it for cover. As Anais advanced around the bay, they moved to positions crouching behind stacked cargo.

Trouble lay just around the corner of the shuttle where the Sekaran had just disappeared. As Anais made her way there, she saw a full unit of Sekarans. At least a dozen of them, and they were ready for her.

Bolt after bolt hit her. It was too much for her nanites to keep up with. Warning signs flashed in her visor, an alarm showing the nanites wouldn't last much longer. Anais rushed back around the corner of the shuttle, putting it between her and the Sekaran soldiers.

She breathed heavily, sweat dripping down her brow despite the climate-controlling features of the nanite armor. There were too many of them. What could she and her team do?

Her companions caught up with her, pressing against the side of the shuttle along with her.

"What's the situation?" Err-dio asked.

"There's a lot of Sekarans around the corner. I don't think they're going to be waiting for us, either. Be ready," Anais said.

Err-dio frowned. He looked to the Arasu. "Head back to the cargo now. We don't want to be caught flat-footed."

They resumed their positions behind the cargo, leaving Anais alone up front. Her nanites slowly recovered, but the power status bar in her visor's vision was still on the low end. She couldn't absorb all that many hits and still survive.

Sekarans came into view. The first would be purely sacrificial. Anais stretched her blade out and hit one has he came into view. Her companions fired their weapons on others. Four Sekarans fell in the first volley, but the rest of them were able to take up positions. They fanned out. Some took cover behind other cargo. Others stayed around the corner, pointing their weapons around toward Anais blindly.

They fired. Anais ducked. She was able to evade the shot from the gun protruding around the corner of the shuttlecraft. In a quick maneuver, she flung her arm upward, slicing at the gun with her light sword. The laser-repeater sparked, the metal slicing off just as easily as her blade cutting through flesh. It fell to the floor, sparks flying everywhere. Anais's wild swing had struck the shuttle as well, leaving a burnt cut in the metal of the craft.

More Sekarans poured out from around the shuttle. Anais couldn't keep up, though she managed to stab her light sword into another one. Laser bolts flew across the room, back and forth between the two groups, but there were too many Sekarans.

Anais fell back to where her friends had taken up their positions. She took a few hits, and her nanite shields flickered out entirely. As more shots flew after her, Anais dove the last steps to slide across the deck and take cover beside Err-dio.

"That didn't look good," Err-dio said, firing his laser-repeater at the oncoming Sekarans.

"It wasn't, "Anais said. "I need to recharge my nanites somehow, or I'm going to be in trouble."

"Drin meditates to do it," Err-dio said.

"I can't really do that here," Anais said.

"Maybe quickly? At least so you have some. I'll cover and prod you if you need to move," Err-dio said.

The shots kept coming. They wouldn't have much time left. Anais closed her eyes, breathed deeply, tried to lessen the tension in her shoulders and neck. It was impossible. She couldn't turn her mind off. She was in too precarious of a situation. *God, help me. I need you.*

Her words sounded desperate in her head, but she felt desperate. She couldn't do this on her own.

Something inside her tingled, like being hit with static electricity when touching a door handle. Anais gasped and opened her eyes.

Her visor showed her nanites had recharged to about fifty percent. How?

"Good timing. They're about to overrun us," Err-dio said.

"We can't retreat," Anais said. "We have to get to the superweapon."

Anais peeked her head up over the cargo pods, trying to spot her other two friends.

One Arasu was dead on the ground, and several of the Sekarans moved in on Fardree. He fought valiantly, taking out one after another as the enemy encroached on his space.

"We'll always be free!" Fardree shouted.

Those were his last words. Two Sekarans broke past his defenses, aiming their rifles at him and blasting him several times. He was hit by so many bolts that his body exploded. Very little remained.

The sight horrified Anais, but the Sekarans turned their full attention to her and Err-dio. They would suffer the same fate soon if they couldn't come up with a plan.

There were just too many of them. In a big, open shuttle bay, what chance did they have?

"Shuttle bay four, we have to launch fighters," someone called through the loudspeaker. "Clear out of the bay or engage your pressure suits. Prepare for decompression."

Alarms blared, sounding in a repetitive rhythm. The forcefield would turn off soon in order to launch shuttles.

Anais was fairly sure she could keep herself alive with her suit, but what about Err-dio? He didn't have a pressure suit. He had to hide somehow. "Get back into the transport!" Anais said.

The laser fire died down as the Sekaran soldiers retreated to a safe place. Err-dio lowered his weapon and glanced back toward their open craft. "Do you think I'll make it?"

"I don't know," Anais said. "But we have to try."

Err-dio nodded and took off running for the transport.

TWENTY-SEVEN

Drin stood on the pad in front of the giant machine. It whirred and pulsed with sound, immense power coursing through it. Light pulsed, blinding Drin's vision. He switched his visor away from its standard mode to get a better view. The device stored an immense amount of energy, enough to take out at least the city above him, perhaps more.

He stood patiently, staring at a large cylinder with controls in an alien language he didn't recognize. Lights flashed and blinked across the machine. Liquid rushed through different translucent tubes. What more could he do? He'd moved to the platform as he'd been called. How would this device work?

Touching the controls wouldn't be a good idea. Drin had seen firsthand how playing with buttons on foreign devices could get one injured or killed. Enough of his Templar brethren had issues with their vipers when they'd first learned to fly. One boy had hit the eject button in the cockpit and was jettisoned into the air. When he fell, his body splattered on the concrete of the training facility. Drin couldn't remember his name, he had been so young, but the sight of the body horrified him and served as a good warning not to do the same.

Lord, Drin prayed, *guide me in what I'm supposed to do.*

The machine kept humming at him, as if daring him to make a move. He could only be cautious to a point. Worlds were at stake, and he had to do his part to fight the Sekaran threat. He couldn't wait here with this machine forever.

Even though it hadn't been more than a few minutes of standing before this machine, Drin found his patience wearing thin. There was too much to think about going on above. Anais fought up in the city—or in space. He couldn't do anything to protect her from here.

"What do you want?" Drin asked aloud. He balled his fist, ready to pound the metal cylinder.

His voice carried through the cavern. Something on the machine blinked. It chirped next, and ancient mechanical devices began to move. They screeched, metal on metal from the thousand years of lying dormant without lubrication. The main cylinder cracked open, along lines Drin didn't spot before it came apart. It revealed another internal device, with a chevron, which turned and unlocked, as well.

Once the layers peeled away, its shell retracting into the platform, it revealed pure energy, with twinkling star-like pulses in its orbit. They moved in a spiral, and it looked much like a model of the universe itself.

Drin stared in awe. The sight captivated him, drew him forward. He could barely keep his body from stumbling into it. The energy reached out to him and pulled him off his feet. Soon, he floated in the air above the platform.

For some reason, he didn't have an urge to fight. This wasn't like the demonic guardians he had just faced. This was something different—there was something pure about this experience. There was no rational way of explaining it. The demons, he'd instinctively known he had to push away as if they were poison, but this—his whole body, mind, and soul desired to open to it.

His nanites receded, the armor shimmering away into nothingness, leaving Drin naked, levitating before the miniature universe.

The energy made a sound as if it were sighing. A beam of light similar to a laser burst toward him, but it did not hurt. The laser scanned Drin from his toes up to his head. He could do nothing but watch as it traced every inch of his body, invading all of his privacy. Nothing would be hidden from this machine.

When it reached Drin's head, it was as if understanding hit him. He was being judged.

The machine wanted to know if Drin was worthy, if he was pure. Did this beam communicate with him? He couldn't tell. It didn't speak to him in the direct sense, but it was as if Drin knew this was a judgment process. Something in his mind activated what had been dormant since birth. The knowledge had always been there, unchanging. How had he not sensed it before?

The beam lingered on his head for several long minutes, with Drin unable to move. Though he was naked, he didn't feel any sensation of cold. Quite the opposite. The machine held him as if he'd been wrapped in a baby swaddle. It brought back memories of his mother and of his youth he had long forgotten. Staring into his mother's eyes. Her staring back. Pure love.

The kind of love he felt for Anais.

The machine made a strange noise when Drin thought of Anais. It reacted as if it were going to buck and throw him off, but it paused. Did the machine pass judgment and then reconsider? Several more moments passed, with Drin helpless before the machine. If there were to be a problem with his judgment, Drin was keenly aware he would die a painful death.

But the machine passed no judgment. It considered Drin's love to be pure.

Another beam of light shot directly into his eyes, this one blinding him. The whole world turned into a white light. Drin struggled, but it was impossible to get free. He felt like he was being sucked out of his own body through his eye sockets, his soul, and essence converted into energy. It was a vacuum so intense, he could do nothing to fight it, though it was immensely painful. If this was to be the end, he hoped God would forgive him for his sins.

The sensation intensified. His eyesight returned, though everything was so vivid and colorful, this wasn't any physical spectrum he'd seen before. The energy in front of him became like a black hole, sucking everything inward, destroying as it consumed. Drin's essence headed directly for the eye of it, the middle. The universe turned and whirled, mesmerizing to Drin. He turned back.

He could see his own body. It dangled in the air. Naked, lifeless. A shell. Drool dripped from his lips. He looked pathetic.

It was a sight he didn't want to see, and so he turned back toward the energy. This was pure beauty. Something to strive to be near. Not like he would have a choice in the matter. He opened himself to it, abandoned his pride, allowed himself to be pulled forward.

Everything turned into a swirl of lights and colors. He circled closer to the epicenter of the energy, and eventually, he faded into it. Each molecule and fiber of his being burst into tiny splinters of light before he evaporated completely. For a long time, the world became darkness. Everything was at peace, still, immutable. There wasn't even a heartbeat.

Before he could get used to this new existence, something changed. Everything changed. It was hard to figure out what had happened at first. Where had he been? Who had he been? He had been a warrior, that much was certain. His memories were still intact, but something blocked them like a closed door. He couldn't quite reach those experiences. There had been a mission, hadn't there? Something important. Lives were at stake.

Birds chirped. Leaves rustled.

Drin opened his eyes.

It was bright outside, a young sun blasting its bright white light across a landscape, washing out many of the colors with its intensity. But his eyes were used to it, they didn't need to adjust. Hadn't he just been somewhere dark?

The air was fresh, easy to breathe, leaves of grass and the surrounding foliage adding a soft scent of life and nature. That was different, too, but it felt very right. Drin took in a deep breath through his nose. The air brought him comfort.

The surrounding area appeared to be a series of rolling hills, with a larger mountain in the distance—still within a day's walk. He could make it there. The mountain was important. He recognized it, but the name of the mountain eluded him. Had he gotten lost from his village? Drin pushed himself to his feet and dusted himself off.

Strange flowing robes adorned him, ones he hadn't remembered dressing in, but they were loose-fitting, and felt natural.

"Are you well, fellow traveler?" a voice asked from behind him.

Drin turned to see a man in plated battle armor, with a sword at his side. He was followed by a dozen men, all of whom looked battle-hardened and ready for more fighting. The tone the man spoke to Drin in was one of kinship. They weren't enemies.

"I'm not certain," Drin said, glancing back at the mountain. "I may have fallen and hit my head. I can hardly remember where I'm from, or where I'm going."

The lead man approached—dark green skin, cool eyes, and a relaxed manner about him. He had a beard that flowed in front of his armor, down to the center of his chest. He approached Drin, his hand moving for Drin's forehead. Drin didn't flinch or recoil. He trusted this man for some reason.

The man touched Drin's temple and held his palm there, a serious expression crossing his face as if he were concentrating. A small glow of pink light radiated from his hand. Warmth flowed through Drin.

His memories came shooting back into his mind as if they'd been fired from a laser-repeater. The sudden wealth of information startled him, causing him to stumble backward, away from the man.

The man didn't seem concerned with Drin's shock. He stood there, watching curiously.

This wasn't right. Drin hadn't been outside on some grassy world with fresh air. He'd been on Arasu, deep in a cavern, with glowing soft light overhead, created by a great machine. He'd activated the machine and fallen into its energy. Thinking about what happened, it sounded strange. It couldn't possibly be real, but here he was. He tried to activate his nanites, to form armor around himself, but nothing happened. Had this man deactivated them somehow? The man's hand glowed. Did he have his own nanites?

Wherever this was, Drin had to get back to Arasu. There was the superweapon. Lives depended on him. Anais. He backpedaled away from the group of men, trying to look for some kind of exit. Was this some sort of holographic display he was caught in? Had he been captured somehow?

"Don't be afraid," the man said in a calm voice, soothing. The voice was distinct and familiar, a deepness to it that would have lulled Drin had the situation not been so strange.

He glanced again toward the mountain. It looked so familiar, but Drin wasn't sure he'd ever been to this location in his life. Where had he been transported to? "Where are you headed?" Drin asked to the bearded man.

The man stepped to Drin's side and pointed to the mountain. "A summit just below the main peak."

"What's there?" Drin asked.

"Destiny."

The wind picked up, blowing across Drin's face. Destiny at the mountain. It hit him. This was the Mount of Alms, the place where The Hundred Years War came to a bloody conclusion. The place where Yezuah brokered peace between the tribes at the cost of his own life. Drin was standing on Eloria.

But Eloria had been overrun by Sekarans centuries ago. His people had fled the world, been purged, their civilization wiped from the land. How could this be? He turned back to the man.

The man locked eyes with Drin. Those eyes were more than just soothing. They were deep, infinite. Drin stifled a breath as he realized he hadn't been looking into the eyes of a man at all.

This was *God*.

The realization made Drin shake. His knees buckled. He found himself prostrate on the ground, face at Yezuah's feet. He dared not even breathe. He kept his head low and tried to remain still.

"I was wondering how long it would take you to recognize me, my son," Yezuah said. "Rise. I told you, you should not be afraid."

Drin exhaled. Men had burst into flames from looking upon their God in the past, but he did not. Still, he would not boast or consider himself worthier than others. This was a blessing or a hallucination. His mind reeled, trying to sort out exactly how he should approach this situation. Yezuah had commanded him to rise, and so he picked himself off the ground once more. His Lord pulled him up by the arm to assist him.

"Better," Yezuah said.

"You know me," Drin said in awe.

"I know all my children."

Drin looked to the twelve behind him. "These are your disciples."

"The founders of my Church. They have done well," Yezuah said. "Or I should say, they will."

"We are in the past then."

"Past, future. Time is a construct of my own making. It means little to me. All is."

Drin nodded, not sure he understood. "What am I supposed to do? Why am I here?"

"The Final Battle approaches," Yezuah said. "As you know, I am going up the hill to die. But I will live again. It is written. My blood will flow to the stars, and all creation will wail and mourn. Until The Final Battle begins, when I will rebuild my kingdom."

"My blade is yours, my Lord," Drin said, lowering his head.

"It is," Yezuah said. "Will you join me then?"

"I am not worthy," Drin said.

"You are my creation," Yezuah said, as if those words should be final. "As is the great machine working through you."

Drin said no more. He didn't need to. He would obey his Lord's command to join him. He couldn't imagine being anywhere else, even though an itch in the back of his mind told him he needed to hurry, for the sake of Arasu—and for Anais. This was a test of patience.

He fell into ranks with the disciples, and he tried not to gawk at them. They were all hardened Elorian warriors, but they had a hopefulness to them, something in their eyes that said they were at peace with themselves, even in the midst of battle. It's what Drin had desired ever since he abandoned the *Justicar* months ago. War had always felt so wrong to him.

But if The Final Battle approached, he would have the opportunity to end it. He had to trust Yezuah, abandon himself to his Lord.

They walked for miles. The disciples laughed together, joked about cultural matters in which Drin had little comprehension. He tried to smile, regardless, and forget the worries he had about the outside world.

"You'll be back in due time, my son," Yezuah said, as if sensing Drin's innermost thoughts.

"Lord, I have something to confess," Drin said, as his return reminded him of Anais. He cared more for protecting her than any other aspect of the coming battle, and guilt welled in him because of it.

"I know your heart, my son. I created man and woman for a purpose."

"But my vows."

"Your vows are fulfilled. You are no longer merely a Templar. You are something more. Be at peace with your feelings."

It was as if a heavy weight lifted from Drin's shoulders. The worry of his feelings for Anais had been eating him up. The stress had been nearly too much for him to handle. But it had changed now. Everything would be different.

They climbed the Mount of Alms, taking a steep ascent. There was no trail along their path. At times, the men had to help each other up to the next ledge, total brotherhood. Drin grabbed onto a rock to try to lift himself up, and nearly slipped, but one of the disciples grabbed him by the wrist and pulled him the rest of the way up.

They wound around the mountain for another hour before reaching the summit. Sweat beaded down Drin's face. He couldn't remember being so hot and tired. It was life without the nanites. He'd grown to rely on them so much when fighting. Another test, perhaps?

They reached the summit. The opposite side of the Mount of Alms had an easy path upward, a simple slope. From this vantage, Drin could see several armies below them. The twelve tribes assembled, and they were all ready to do battle, to spill blood.

"Now, we wait," Yezuah said.

Drin wanted to change history, to take the burden from his Lord, but he knew he couldn't. Yezuah's sacrifice cleansed all

Elorians of the wages of sins. Even though his Lord was calm about it, it wasn't fair to him. The pain he would endure in moments. The disciples had no clue. They were joking around like this were any other day. Soon, their worlds would change forever.

Drin recalled the verses in the Holy Book, where Yezuah's blood had spilled. It sounded so painful. It was the slaughter of an innocent. Senseless. And it was coming.

An army approached from the clearing below. The time of reckoning would be soon.

Unlike modern battles, the commander stood at the front. Drin recognized the long face and thick brows, which signified a member of the Dawn tribe. The cast-out tribe of Eloria, the non-believers who betrayed Yezuah.

The commander's name was Pylah, depicted in paintings and plays as a tragic figure, a man who went mad because of what he'd realized he'd done. All Drin could do was to watch and wait. Yezuah had brought him here to see this for a reason.

"General Yezuah?" Pylah said. His cold eyes glanced over Yezuah. The Dawn tribe commander was much bigger than Drin's Lord. He had a thick torso and arms, sturdy, warlike. Yezuah was nimble and much smaller by comparison. If they had fought a duel, it wouldn't be a fair one.

But they wouldn't fight a duel. "Just Yezuah. The time for fighting among our peoples has ended, and thus, I no longer require the title of general," Yezuah said. "I've come to broker peace and to bring the tribes together. It will last for a thousand years and more."

"You would lead this peace?" Pylah asked.

"I will."

"You're delusional," Pylah said. "My full army is behind me, and you only bring a handful of men? The arrogance of what you're doing!" Pylah belly-laughed.

It wasn't arrogance, it was humility. Yezuah was offering

himself to end the war. No one knew it at the time. No one could see it. Even though their Lord had warned them. Drin tried to fight tears. He didn't want to distract Pylah or the others. He was here as an observer, nothing more. None seemed to take note of him, despite the sinking feeling inside his gut. This wasn't fair, nor right.

"I forgive you," Yezuah said. "You and I will sit together one day, and you will find peace. This is the only assurance I can offer you for now."

"You're insane." Pylah clutched his knife by his side.

Drin would have rushed forward and stopped him, at least jumped in front of Yezuah, and absorbed the coming attack. But he couldn't. The salvation of the entire galaxy was on the line. Yezuah had trusted him to observe, to understand his sacrifice.

The other disciples were caught completely off guard. Pylah rushed forward and drove his knife directly into Yezuah's gut, twisting and yanking to the side to further tear at his insides. It would have been excruciating. Yezuah clenched his jaw but did not scream. He merely looked at Pylah in the eyes.

"For the Dawn!" Pylah said, but his voice quivered.

"A new dawn is coming," Yezuah said, collapsing into his enemy's arms.

Pylah dropped the knife, holding onto Yezuah. "Why don't you fight back?" Tears streaked down his face.

Yezuah's blood spilled on the ground. The world shook violently, a quake like Drin had never experienced before. He couldn't keep his footing. A large crack opened in the ground behind Pylah. The man's heel hit where the ground gave way, and he lost his balance, releasing Yezuah in the process.

Yezuah's body hit the ground. He convulsed there. Pylah fell backward into the crack formed by the shaking. The quake still hadn't stopped. Would the whole world fall apart? It was the will of the Lord which held the very fabric of existence together, and the Lord was dead.

Pylah fell into the crack, the earth swallowing him. He grabbed onto the ledge for dear life.

One of the disciples, Gian, the one whom Yezuah loved, stepped forward. He grabbed his enemy by the wrist and pulled him out of the crumbling rock and dirt, bringing him to safety.

"Why?" Pylah asked.

"It's what my Lord would have done," Gian said.

Drin rushed forward toward Yezuah, tears streaking down his face. He'd read about the scene many times, seen it depicted in holos, but nothing prepared him for actually watching the great love Yezuah displayed for his enemy in person, as well as for his followers. It was too much to bear. He shouldn't have had to sacrifice himself this way.

He turned Yezuah over, but the bearded man was already bleeding out. His eyes were open, vacant pools, but still containing the depths of eternity. As his life left him, the pools seemed to grow into a monstrous light. Fire. Creation and destruction all at once.

"It's finished," Yezuah muttered.

Light exploded from his eyes. Drin had to recoil and place his hand in front of his face. The energy engulfed him and everything around him. The world washed out into nothingness.

TWENTY-EIGHT

Anais wished she had something better to grip onto from where she was seated.

Err-dio manned the piloting station of the shuttlecraft while the Sekarans bombarded it with laser fire. "It doesn't look like we have any weapons at our disposal on this transport," he said, a perplexed look crossing his face as he tapped controls frantically. The door was sealed behind them, keeping them safe, in a sense.

"Can we fire the engines? Ram them?" Anais asked.

Err-dio shook his head. "We slaved the system to the mothership's AI when we landed. We can't launch without them releasing us. A safety protocol."

"Damn," Anais said. She bit her lip, watching through the cockpit windshield as the Sekarans pelted them. They'd break through the ship's hull eventually, or blow up the craft's engines. Either way, they only had minutes to live unless they came up with a plan. "I don't think I have the ability to fend them all off. Drin could, I'm sure, but I can't fight like him," she said.

Err-dio nodded, spinning in the pilot's chair toward her. "I know."

Anais looked out the windshield. The Sekarans had finished moving the superweapon. They had set it up in the corner of the shuttle bay. Engineers attached wires to it. They appeared to be getting ready to fire the weapon from the shuttlebay to destroy the Araisu planet. This wasn't good at all. Time was running out. "We have to do something."

"We need more firepower," Err-dio said.

Anais shook her head. What could she do? There were other fighters in the bay...

"Wait," she said.

"Hmm?"

"If I got you to one of the Sekaran fighters, do you think you could rig it to activate their weapons?" Anais asked.

"I suppose so, but I don't see how we'll survive... Oh!" His eyes went wide. "Survival doesn't matter. We have one mission, which is far more crucial. You are wise, Sister Anais."

Goosebumps formed on her arms. She hadn't heard Err-dio refer to her as *sister* before. It felt right. The effects of this religion never ceased to bring her wonders. *God, you'd better be with us now,* she thought.

"I'm going to see if I can bring you into my nanite's shield bubble, and then we'll get you over to the closest fighter," Anais said. She hoped it would work, and that her shields could last long enough to be effective.

"A good plan. My compliments," Err-dio said.

"Don't praise me just yet," Anais said. She activated her nanite shield, focusing, hoping she could make it extend beyond herself to another. The nanites pushed out, energy flickering in the air. They surrounded Err-dio. It was working!

Her elation died as quickly as it had come, as the Sekarans smashed through the cockpit's windshield with their laser bolts. Anais ducked, even though there was nothing in danger of hitting her. They had to move quickly, however, or the next shots would hit them.

She hit the control pad to lower the ramp, bracing herself for more fire from the Sekarans who were no doubt outside of the vessel.

Five soldiers stood at the bottom, waiting for them. They opened fire, bolts ramming into Anais' shield.

"Let's go! Stay with me," Anais said. She rushed forward, hoping Err-dio would remain within her shield's capacities. Her light sword penetrated the armor of one Sekaran, and then another. The confusion caused them to stop hitting her for a brief moment, enough for Anais to identify the location of a nearby fighter and a path toward it.

A Sekaran with a light sword stepped in her path. They clashed blades, their energy sparking, causing the other Sekarans to backpedal away from them. She tried to position herself so the Sekaran would act as another shield between them, but she had little choice, trying to keep Err-dio protected and yet make her way toward the fighter.

The Sekaran swung his blade across her torso. Anais jumped backward, sucking her stomach in. It barely missed her. She could feel the heat from it. It had been close, even with her nanite protection. Light blades could do much more damage than a standard laser repeater.

The attack threw her off balance, and the Sekaran pushed her backward into Err-dio. The Skree grabbed onto her with his extra arms, keeping her steady and upright. Without him, she would have fallen onto her rear, and she was grateful for the assist. But she couldn't keep getting pushed back like this. Several laser bolts hit her, her shield power diminishing. She couldn't stay locked in combat forever with this swordsman.

She tried to push her attack forward, whacking with her blade, a lot less elegantly than either this Sekaran or Drin would have.

Her opponent parried gracefully, using footwork to slip by her and kick her in the thigh.

It caused her to stumble backward again, but this time, Err-dio wasn't there.

She glanced to the side, distracted. It was a bad movie because, out the corner of her eye, she could see the Sekaran bringing his blade down toward her. Err-dio had managed to get out of the way, maneuvering around her shielding. He positioned himself carefully, using the Sekaran and her as cover from the others while leveling his laser-repeater at Anais's opponent.

Err-dio fired, blowing the Sekaran's head off. The helpless body twitched a few times before losing its grip on its light sword, which clanked to the ground. The point-blank murder shocked the other Sekarans, who momentarily stopped firing. This was their window.

"Go!" Anais said.

The two of them rushed the fighter. Laser fire resumed, pelting the back of her shield. The cockpit of the fighter was open, awaiting a Sekaran pilot to hop inside. It was a little higher up than they could climb easily, but they didn't need to, did they?

She couldn't take too many more hits, but they were so close. Err-dio returned fire, but on the run, his shots proved inaccurate. He only managed to strike one Sekaran soldier. With the dozens approaching them, it did little good.

They reached the base of the fighter. Err-dio moved for the ladder. "No, we'll never make it that way," Anais said. "Grab onto me."

Err-dio looked confused, but he wrapped arms around her waist and clung to her. His grip proved a little too tight, as it hampered Anais's breathing, but she didn't have time to complain. She hoped the nanites had enough power left to give her a good boost. It would be their only shot. If they spent time climbing the ladder, her shields would have failed.

She bent her knees and jumped into the air. Laser bolts smashed into the deck and crates behind her, where they had been a moment prior. Her jump sent her and Err-dio close to the top of the tall ceiling of the shuttle bay, but they descended in perfect line with the cockpit seats.

When she landed, Anais stumbled, but only into the cockpit dash. She hoped she hadn't touched any wrong controls in the process, but it didn't seem to do anything.

"Sit down," Err-dio said, slipping into the main seat. Anais took the co-piloting chair behind. The fighter was designed for three, with one seat for a rear gunner so the Sekarans could shoot multi-directionally. The hatch closed atop her a moment later, her long ears brushing against it. She was a little taller than was comfortable for her spot, and so she slumped into the seat.

Err-dio worked frantically. "I have to try to override their controls. I've worked Sekaran vehicles before, but there are security keys. Perhaps I can bypass..." He didn't finish his thought but ripped open the panel, exposing several colorful and glowing wires as well as a bank of crystal chits. Anais had no idea what any of them did, but Err-dio worked with incredible speed, pulling out wires, moving chits to different locations.

In the meantime, the Sekarans opened fire on their own vessel. This one was a little more robust than the transport, a fighter meant for war. The hull wouldn't fail them, or so she hoped.

With a *guh-zee*, the shuttlecraft powered on. Laser bolts went from hitting the hull to smashing into an energy shield.

"You did it!" Anais said.

"Not yet," Err-dio said. He grabbed onto a joystick, which shifted his display to a targeting computer, complete with camera. He honed in on the Sekaran superweapon. If the Sekarans managed to get a shot off, millions might die.

Err-dio locked the lasers on the weapon and pulled the trigger. The superweapon exploded, bursting into millions of bits, sparks, and flames flying everywhere. The Sekaran engineers and gunners around the device either burned or were thrown away the blast.

"Woo!" Anais said, reaching over and squeezing Err-dio's shoulders. She wanted to hug him, but it was the best she could do from her position.

Err-dio let out a big breath of relief. "I hope they didn't find more of these devices."

"Way to kill the moment," Anais said, wrinkling her nose. They had won a big victory, one that had seemed impossible before. But Err-dio was right, this wasn't the only superweapon the Sekarans had used against a planet. She could only hope that they didn't have immediate access to more.

Before they could celebrate further, red lights flashed in the cargo bay. An alarm wailed.

"What's going on?" Anais asked. "Did we draw too much attention?"

Err-dio looked at the control screen. "No, it doesn't have to do with us," he said. "A general alarm. The Sekarans are calling for evacuation."

Evacuation? Was the ship taking hits from outside? The Elorians must have gotten to them. Their timing was good. If they had been able to get their superweapon online, it would have tipped the scale of the battle.

But now they were in an equally dangerous situation. Sekarans flooded into the shuttle bay.

TWENTY-NINE

DRIN BREATHED IN DEEPLY. THE FRESHNESS OF THE AIR ON ancient Eloria had given way to a stale, moldy scent. The cave. He was back on Arasu, with the great machine and all its glory. Where the light had been moments earlier, he now stood, gazing out upon the entire cavern. It was bright around him. The glowing seemed to radiate...from himself?

He glanced downward.

His body shimmered, bright, radiating in light and energy. It had a translucent look to it, almost like a ghost. It startled Drin.

Were the nanites acting strangely after interacting with this great machine? He tried to will the nanites to change appearance, away from his armored appearance to general robed clothing. They shimmered, and the clothes changed, but the translucency of his skin didn't change. His body had become something else. What had happened?

He wiggled his fingers, moved his arms. Everything seemed to work normally, but he felt much lighter than usual. His movements didn't carry any weight to them.

The machine rumbled, energy flowing through it. All of the

energy seemed to course through Drin's veins. Each breath was an exhilaration, a greater high than he'd ever experienced. He was one with this energy, and with the entire planet. He could sense everything from the hot magma core to all of the cities up above, the insectoid creatures moving and buzzing, tickling like they were small bugs on his skin. What a strange world. A part of him, for now.

The sensations were so strange. What if he couldn't get back to normal? What if he were stuck here forever?

Don't be afraid.

The voice came from his head, but it wasn't his own.

"Who's there?" Drin asked.

I am who I am.

Those words. They had been said when the Lord appeared to many others. Back on Eloria, he'd looked into Yezuah's eyes, into those pools, the light and the energy flooded into him. The same as the machine had done here. What was going on?

He took a deep breath. First, he would have to leave the center of this machine, if he could. He hadn't attempted to move yet. He pushed forward, but the air condensed around him, like a wall. He couldn't move from this spot. He was trapped.

You are my vessel now. Stop resisting. The flesh is no longer your world.

The words made Drin's hair stand on his neck. He wasn't ready for this. He had so much to do still. There was a war going on, and he hadn't reported to the Templars beyond a brief call to the cardinal. Anais and Err-dio were out there, counting on him to return. If he couldn't be flesh, how could he help them?

He found himself shaking. This was too much too fast. He'd not been prepared for this. He wasn't complete enough to be God's vessel.

I've prepared you from the moment you were born. Don't be afraid.

It kept being repeated to him, and the words had warmth to them, but Drin wasn't so sure. How could he be sure this was God and not some kind of trick?

The voice didn't answer him this time. Doubt. He knew better. The miracles of the nanites and what they provided for the Templars were evidence enough of God's great work. He had to believe in this. It was much the same strange technology that appeared to be magic to the untrained eye. This was how God chose to communicate to his people. Drin had to accept it, to get past his doubts and fears. Those only clouded his mind and his purpose.

"I'm sorry," Drin said. His voice cracked, and it echoed throughout the cavern.

Time passed, silence.

"I said I'm sorry," Drin said.

You're forgiven. Patience. I am with you.

Drin took in a deep breath, centering himself and clearing his thoughts. His breathing exercises were designed for the pressures of this situation. He could get through this. He had his God with him. It was an honor beyond what anyone else had ever experienced. Even the disciples didn't have this intimate connection. "I am yours, Lord. Guide me with your steady hand and lead me," Drin said.

The cavern shook, rocks falling from overhead. It began to collapse. Drin tried to run again from his place within the great machine but, again, the very air in front of him stopped him, held him in as if it were a prison cell.

The ceiling collapsed, and water rose up the platform. He watched as rocks crashed into the two pods which had held those demons. They sparked and exploded, causing even more violent shakes within the cave. A pillar fell, and everything started to collapse.

"I need to get out of here," Drin cried. "Lord, please."

Your faith is so little. Did you think I would allow harm to come to my vessel?

The cave kept collapsing in on itself, but the column of air surrounding Drin was kept safe. No rocks passed through it, just like Drin couldn't leave it. It left one column safe as the caved-in ceiling filled in all around him. Drin's cell was the only location to survive. There was still light, allowing him to see because it was radiating from his body. But how would he get out of here?

Trust.

Drin nodded. "I want to. I don't know how."

Good.

The first step to repentance was to admit the problem. To admit that the self was not going to be the answer to all the problems. He needed God. He had to rely fully on Him. It had always been the answer in the past, it would always be the answer in the future. It was the answer.

Drin closed his eyes.

Now believe.

He had to get out of this cavern if he was to be any good to anyone. It was his duty to do the Lord, and he would do so. If his corporeal form had disappeared, then he wouldn't be bound by such flesh, would he? Was that what the Lord meant by telling him to believe?

He focused. Faith was everything. Faith could move mountains, caves, change the very world around him. He'd seen it done so many times.

A picture of the surface formed in his mind. The large canyon where he'd landed his viper. Hopefully, the ship hadn't washed away when the rushing water had flooded the canyon.

You don't need to rely on worldly devices.

Right. Drin exhaled again, and he pictured himself out of his claustrophobic enclosure. He willed it. The Lord was with him, and he had to be out of here.

The picture became clearer in his mind. The hot sun, the dry river bed. A cave entrance in the distance and the Arasu city encased in the rock face beyond it. He recalled it vividly. The air seemed to change again. Dusty, dry, not like Eloria or the cave.

He opened his eyes.

It wasn't a cool, dark cave anymore. He'd transported himself to the surface of Arasu. His viper wasn't there anymore—it had been washed away, just as he had feared. Several metal panel scraps lay on the ground, remnants of his former ship and former life. The sight made him sad. He'd been through so much in that tiny little ship.

It didn't matter. Attachments to physical things came from pride, not God. He had to move on. From both the ship and from his own fleshly body.

He didn't dare look down at himself again, for fear he didn't have a corporeal form. It wasn't necessary right now. He had other matters to accomplish.

Sekarans on skybikes and ground transports rushed past him. They were headed to the city, no doubt. But that was, again, a minor worry. Something he could deal with later, once he solved the actual problem.

He turned his attention skyward. Debris clouds and explosions littered the atmosphere, vibrant in the evening sky. Night had fallen over the world while he'd been in the cavern. How long had it been? Days? Hours? There was no way of telling. But it didn't matter. The battle above was epic, and even though Drin didn't have a tactical computer, it was clear the Sekaran and Elorian fleets had met here. This battle would determine the course of more than just one world.

And it wasn't going well for the Templars. He could sense that much, as well. The Sekarans were too numerous, too powerful.

The Elorians needed his help. They needed God's help.

Drin closed his eyes and prayed.

THIRTY

"WHAT DO WE DO?" ANAIS ASKED.

"Pray," Err-dio said.

Easier said than done. She could hardly focus on anything except for the Sekarans flooding into the shuttle bay. Some were climbing the ladder to their cockpit. If they managed to open it, she and Err-dio were finished.

"We need to go," Anais said. She was too nervous to close her eyes and be in the calm space Drin would have been in had he been in this very situation. She clutched the seat in front of her tightly, her fingers digging into the fabric of the pilot's chair.

Err-dio messed with controls, working at speeds to where Anais couldn't even see what was going on. She trusted him. He'd been able to get them out of jams several times before.

"Got it!" Err-dio said finally. Their fighter began to turn.

Two Sekarans in pressurized battle armor had climbed the ladder on the side, and they started banging on the cockpit hatch. Anais yelped when a fist came all too close to her head, even though she was sealed inside, away from her enemy.

The shuttle bay had been depressurized during their time

trying to get the fighter to work. Whether it was intentionally from the Sekarans, or they lost power to their forcefield systems, Anais couldn't tell.

Err-dio pushed the thrust forward, jolting Anais back into her seat. The fighter took off and the Sekarans fell off it. Better now than when they were out in the middle of space.

The ship shot out of the shuttle bay and into the great battle.

Laser blasts covered the starred backdrop ahead of them. Anais looked up, and it appeared much the same. It looked like the bulk of the Elorian and Sekaran fleets had arrived here. Debris flew everywhere. Dozens of smaller ships floated in space with no power, others looked like they were about to explode. Fighters chased each other. Capital ships fired their much larger weapons. The sight was unlike anything Anais had ever seen.

Their ship rocked. Anais glanced behind her to see another Sekaran fighter had followed them out of the shuttle bay. It kept up with them no matter how Err-dio attempted to maneuver away from it. He twisted the ship in between large debris from destroyed vessels, but it kept up with them. At least, he managed to evade most of their weapons' fire.

"You're going to have to get into the third seat and manage the rear gunning station," Err-dio said.

Anais looked over her shoulder. She could see the controls, a targeting display, but it was all foreign to her. "I don't know how it works."

"Use the targeting display. Move the gun until it locks on the target. You'll know when you see it. Then squeeze the trigger and fire!"

This seemed like a bad plan, but she didn't have a better one. She unstrapped herself, shimmying out of the harness straps before turning to make her way over her seat. As she moved, Err-dio tilted the shuttle again in a tight turn. Anais went flying into the hatch and sidewall, thudding against it. The jolt shook her to her core and would leave a bruise on her shoulder. She winced. "Keep still!"

"Not if you want to survive," Err-dio said.

She couldn't fault him for maneuvering out of enemy fire. She just had to get herself into the seat before he needed to dodge again.

The moment came sooner than she could have anticipated after she'd pushed her legs over the back of the seat. This time, Err-dio jerked them upward, forcing her to fall forward into the controls. She used the gunning controls as a brace, accidentally firing several wild shots while she stabilized herself. The controls jutted toward her, and she gripped the joystick by both hands, sliding into the seat. Then, she reached up to strap herself in. It wouldn't do to be flying all over the place when Err-dio made another maneuver.

The targeting display made a representation of what was going on outside, easier for a gunner to read without having all of the stray debris and everything else in a battle cluttering the vision. It showed different heat and movement signatures and allowed her to easily zoom in on her current location, where she spotted the Sekaran ship following them.

The controls proved a little more difficult to navigate. They had two handles, under which each of her fingers rested on a pull trigger. She could tilt the controls on a 3-D axis, but as she moved, she found the Sekaran was one step ahead of keeping her off a lock on his ship.

A laser blast hit the left tail of their fighter. Anais yelped as the blast connected with their ship through the shielding. It could have very well hit her.

"I can't shake him much longer," Err-dio said.

"I'm trying!" Anais snapped back.

She may have been a little hard on Err-dio, for all he'd done to keep them alive so far, but these targeting controls were beyond frustrating. Any minuscule movement caused the guns to swing wildly. It was all she could do to keep it steady.

If only the nanites could take over her reflexes, give her supernatural ability like they did in strength and speed.

Could they? They seemed capable of most other things: night vision, creating weapons from thin air, healing. Why wouldn't they be able to assist her in targeting?

She closed her eyes, breathing in deeply and exhaling in the way Drin taught her. Calm. Focus. Nothingness. Only from that state could she really control the little machines flowing through and around her. She willed them to assist her vision, her fingers, her arm strength. To keep her steady, to guide her aim so it would be true. Her eyes fluttered open to the sound of more blasts. The hits came closer. She had to act—now or never.

Narrowing her eyes on the target, Anais adjusted her movements ever so slightly. The guns angled up and to the right. The target came into the crosshairs. Anais squeezed the triggers.

Dual laser blasts fired from turrets in the rear of her ship. They continued as Anais held the triggers down. She dared to look up into the night sky, and as she did, she caught the explosive blast of a ship being hit squarely by laser fire. She'd done it! The Sekaran ship had been destroyed!

"I got him!" Anais exclaimed.

"Good work," Err-dio said.

Anais glanced toward the front of the cockpit. His controls flashed a bright red, their light pulsing on his skin. He moved about his piloting controls frantically. Whatever was going on couldn't be good, and Anais didn't dare interrupt his concentration.

They flew by a large Elorian ship. It appeared much like the *Justicar*, a brief home for Anais where she had learned to use her nanites for healing.

They headed right in the path of the large Elorian vessel.

"We're going to crash into the ship!" Anais said.

"The Sekarans managed to hit one of our rear engines," Err-dio said. "I'm having trouble maneuvering."

To make matters worse, the Elorian ship directed its weapons at them. Dozens of laser bolts flew in their direction. Anais' eyes went wide. They were in a Sekaran fighter. The Elorians thought they were the enemy!

Several of the bolts connected with the front shielding of the ship, hitting them with enough force to throw off their trajectory. Taking fire saved them. They missed colliding with the Elorian ship's hull, running parallel with it as they came close.

Another Sekaran ship appeared in Anais's view, the bigger target, firing its main cannons on the Elorians. It connected, a solid beam dragging across the hull, doing catastrophic damage to the Elorians. The sight made Anais wince, as parts and bodies flew out into space. But it had been a blessing—the Elorians no longer fired upon her tiny ship. One more hit might have destroyed them.

Err-dio pulled up, trying to get away from the Elorian capital ship. He managed to get them some breathing room, but they collided with some of the debris being flung from the Sekarans' weapons fire. The jolt shook the ship and sent it into a tailspin. The rapid turning made Anais want to vomit, but she managed to hold it in. Her vision went blurry from dizziness.

The ship stabilized from its spinning, but Err-dio slammed his fists on the piloting controls. "It's broken," he said.

"Can you fix it?"

"Not from here."

The ship moved on a forward trajectory, toward Arasu. The planet grew to encompass everything around them. They were headed for the atmosphere.

Anais clutched her targeting controls tightly but snuck a glance behind her. "Do something!"

"I would if I could," Err-dio said.

The situation escalated in danger as they entered Arasu's atmosphere. If they came in at the wrong trajectory, they could burn up. As they descended, the shields absorbed most of the energy, but the nose of the craft began to melt. It turned red hot.

The jolting made Anais have to right herself in her seat, forcing her to gaze out into space and the battle beyond. She couldn't see what was happening with the main battle. Her ship fell further and further into Arasu's sky. Perhaps it would be better this way. If they burned up or crashed and disintegrated, she wouldn't feel the moment of her death.

It was something that had worried her since she was a little girl —dying. Every day, she got older, her body decayed. There was nothing she could do to prevent it. Eventually, her body would fail her, or she would have some accident. No matter what, it sounded painful—excruciating as she imagined herself gasping for her last breath, not wanting to disappear into oblivion. Inevitable darkness. God, she didn't want to be thinking about it now. There had to be some way out of this mess.

The ship maintained its descent. They passed through clouds, which meant they were far enough into the atmosphere where burn-up wouldn't be a risk. At least, they'd evaded that fate, but if they hit the ground at these speeds, would it matter?

Err-dio fumbled with controls. "I'm sorry, Anais. I've failed in protecting you," he said.

"Don't be sorry. We did everything we could. At least the superweapon is destroyed. We made a difference, right?" Anais asked.

They'd been prepared for a suicide mission when they entered the Sekaran battleship. It was amazing she and Err-dio made it out alive. They'd had a good run. She'd been able to save billions of lives from her efforts. It counted.

"You're right," Err-dio said. "It was an honor to fight with you."

"And you, my friend."

Err-dio began muttering prayers to himself. Anais couldn't make out the words, but she figured she should do the same. The ground would be approaching soon. She closed her eyes. *Please, God. I want to be in Heaven with you, with my family. Make me clean.* She wasn't sure if that was the best way to pray, but it felt right.

Her mind drifted to Drin. His muscular form, deep eyes, green skin. She would never be able to see him again, and for that reason alone, it pained her heart. Tears streaked down her face. It would all be over in a moment. Her life had been a blessing, all things considered. Yes. She was ready to die.

"Drin..." the word escaped her lips. If he was out there, some-where, she hoped he wouldn't forget her.

THIRTY-ONE

Drin...

The voice came through like a whisper in his ear. He could hear the softness in the voice, the love, the tenderness. It filled him with an intense sensation that would have been akin to a shiver if he still maintained a corporeal form.

"Anais," he said. Could she hear him similarly? With the way the machine's energy interacted with his nanites, it boosted all of their abilities. She had a connection with him through the nanites.

He reached out for her, spreading his essence across the planet. Though he could see everywhere, he still maintained the limitations of man. It was impossible to process all of the data being input all at once. He had to focus his search for her.

He struck out in a narrow beam of energy, jutting across the sky of Arasu, twisting and turning to try to find her. To those below, he would appear as a pillar of light, passing through the landscape.

A Sekaran craft appeared in the sky. It was badly damaged, suffering from too much heat from reentry, as well as smoke rising from its engines. It appeared to be out of control.

At first, Drin thought to ignore the craft. What did he care what happened to Sekarans? But his instincts told him he should investigate the matter. He let his essence drift toward the craft. To his surprise, it wasn't a Sekaran piloting the fighter, but a Skree. Drin reached further into the cockpit, and there he spotted Anais.

He wanted to tell her not to worry, but she had already passed out from descending into the atmosphere too quickly. The strain from the g-forces had been too much for her, and Err-Dio, as well, judging from the way he slumped forward. But they were still breathing. They still had their lives' essences.

"I'll protect you, Anais," Drin said, even though she couldn't hear him. Perhaps in her delirious state, her nanites could communicate to her.

He willed more of his essence toward the craft, cradling it, as if in his palm, as it descended. In this form, and with the speeds it was traveling, he couldn't hold it in place, but he was able to guide it with the energy flowing through him.

The fighter fell at a much slower rate, Drin providing extra resistance to slow it down even further as it came close to the surface. He guided it into the main canyon, so it would land near to the Arasu city he'd seen before. They would need medical attention when they arrived, and Drin was in no position to be able to provide it for them at the moment.

The craft landed softly, a better landing than Err-dio could have performed had he had control of the ship. Drin smiled at his work. This was truly a blessing from Yezuah. So much power at his disposal, all for the glory of God.

He still didn't have a complete harness on the power. Wind picked up, causing much of Drin's essence to dissipate in the air. He needed to reform to be whole again. The energy of his soul scattered, but as he focused, it drew back together. The act was very tiring. By the time he recomposed himself, he wanted nothing but to be able to rest.

There is much more to do, my son.

Yezuah was still with him. He could hear God's commands directly. And he had to act. "Your will be done," Drin said.

Your faith is still little, like a seed, and it must grow. Believe in my goodness, Drin. You can do anything.

It was much the same message displayed throughout the Holy Book. With God, nothing was beyond his limits. He and the other Templars had recited such verses as platitudes. It felt good to say them, but he had never truly considered what it meant, how big God was, how infinite His reach. Faith was said to be able to move mountains, to stop tides. Drin had always considered those to be metaphors, but what if it meant so much more? What if he could bend reality through faith alone?

He had to try. For the good of all creation. God commanded him, after all.

Drin cleared his mind, meditating on the goodness of God, the sacrifice Yezuah made for all. He could do anything through the Lord. That included returning to his flesh, did it not? It would be an interesting test.

He focused all of his energy, recalling what it was like to be himself, to walk on his own feet, to stretch his arms, and see through his own eyes. His energy whirled in a circle, gaining momentum like a cyclone until, finally, bright lights and sparks fell around him, and he was Drin again. An Elorian. Two hands, two feet, he was all there, standing atop a ledge overlooking a great canyon below. He stepped close to the edge, having no fear of falling. He could dissipate and reform himself again at will. This machine made his nanotechnology complete. He was one with them now.

Explosions filled the sky above. A battle of epic proportions. Drin had much to do, and he couldn't waste time pontificating his form. He'd be able to do that later. For now, he had to ascertain what was going on above.

He let his body shatter into energy, lifting himself up off the surface of Arasu. The planet did not bind him any more than his body did. He raised his essence into the upper atmosphere and beyond. Vacuum could not harm his non-corporeal form. He no longer required air. His faith had truly set him free.

His essence spread across the battle above. The Elorians had six destroyers, four light cruisers, two heavy cruisers, and a full fighter carrier in the system. Thousands of tinier dots circled each other in an intense dog fight with Sekaran fighters. The fighter combat alone would be one of the bloodiest in history if it hadn't been already.

The Sekarans, meanwhile, had five dreadnoughts, three destroyers, and six cruisers. Drin couldn't distinguish the ships beyond that, as he hadn't studied Sekaran ship design like he had the Elorians. They appeared to all be heavily armed, firing laser weapons and projectiles at a rapid pace.

From the look of the battle, the Sekarans were winning. Though the Sekarans had one of their capital ships adrift in space, the Elorians had three, which were heavily damaged. If the Sekarans managed to incapacitate a couple more, the Elorians would face too much focused fire to be able to combat their advances.

It wasn't good.

For a while, Drin watched, surveying the battle. All this power and he didn't know how to utilize it. He could only watch as his people took massive casualties, even as they inflicted many upon the Sekarans. It was much like the battle where the *Justicar* had fallen prey to a Sekaran trap. This appeared to be another one.

He scanned for the superweapon. Such a monstrosity would produce far more energy than regular weapons, but it didn't appear to be anywhere within the fleet. Had the Sekarans loaded it onto one of their vessels and run? No, it wouldn't make sense with the bulk of the fighting here. They would have wanted to use it on the Elorian ships and end this battle easily. Whoever prevailed here would have a big advantage on the galactic stage.

A Sekaran dreadnought fired its main guns, blasting a beam directly through the center of an Elorian ship. Another one down. He couldn't worry about the superweapon. Anais and Err-dio had been set to the task of destroying it. They wouldn't have left the battle and failed, would they?

He had to have faith in his people, as much as he had in God's plan. His task here would be for something much greater. He had to change the course of this battle.

But how? He approached one of the Sekaran vessels, let his essence flow into it. What he could do was to reform his corporeal-self on one of the bridges.

He did so.

The Sekarans panicked as a bright light winked into the bridge, and suddenly there was an Elorian.

Drin formed a light sword in his hand. The bridge was a large circular pit on the Sekaran ship. The captain shouted orders, pointing at Drin. He would be Drin's first target.

Several of the Sekarans fired laser-repeaters at him, but they had little effect. He walked up to the captain, keeping his strides steady, calm. His confidence shook the enemy. One crewman tried to jump in the way, but Drin cut him in half immediately, not sparing a second on his way toward the captain.

The Sekaran captain tried to backpedal and run. Like a game. "I'll give you a chance to repent your ways and leave this battle. Confess that Yezuah is the Lord God, and you will be allowed to live," Drin said.

"Never, infidel!" the captain spat.

"So be it," Drin said. Laser bolts hit him in the back, but they dissipated in his new energy form. His enemies could do nothing to him. He doubted even a battle mage would be able to stop him now.

The captain dodged Drin's advance, hiding behind a console in the center of the room. Drin leaped over it with ease. He grabbed the captain by the tunic, pulling him close. Then he drove his light sword through the captain's belly. The Sekaran's eyes went dull, and Drin tossed the body aside.

The next few moments turned the Sekaran bridge into a slaughterhouse. It was much like when Drin first visited the planet Nemayr. None of these Sekarans stood a chance against him. His mere presence had disrupted them to where they couldn't perform their duties.

But this time, Drin understood that it was a mercy to end their lives, so they wouldn't cause more harm. It was war, both physical and spiritual. The true enemy had a grasp upon their souls, tendrils intertwined in their veins, running through their hearts. He could do nothing for them other than stop the poisonous spread of their evil throughout the galaxy.

One by one, he felled the Sekarans on the bridge, until there were none left. Drin frowned, seeing the bodies everywhere. The death didn't fill him with joy. It couldn't. He would have preferred mercy if there were another way. But the Sekarans would have none of it. They wouldn't stop until the last one of them was dead. To save the rest of the galaxy, Drin had to do his duty. No matter how it felt.

He turned non-corporeal once more, allowing his essence to drift back out to the overall battle. The removal of one ship's officers helped the Elorians to regroup. They weren't in immediate danger, but the Sekarans moved again to flank them. If they succeeded, his people would be in worse shape than even before.

Going through each ship one at a time and personally dispatching their leadership wouldn't do. It would take too long. Elorians would die in the process. He had to come up with another solution, and quickly.

You can do anything, my son.

The voice again. Hadn't he been doing what he was told? Wasn't this a leap of faith, being able to cast off his physical form and reappear anywhere with a thought? What more could God want of him?

The voice went silent. It was for Drin to figure out on his own. God was so much bigger than this battle. He had an entire universe to manage. To Him, this must have looked like tiny insects, buzzing about each other. None of it could harm God, despite the havoc the Sekarans wreaked upon His creation.

An idea struck Drin. That was it. God was bigger than all of this. God was infinite. Drin had been thinking about the scope of the battle and his own abilities in too small a form. If he truly were God's son, as he put it, he could do so much more than this. He could be bigger as well.

Lord, bless what I am about to do. Let me bring peace to your people and to your creation, and have mercy on the souls I must fell in the process.

Drin focused himself once more. He spread his essence out, grew it, replicating himself to cast himself as a giant looking down upon this scene. Soon he grew to where the ships were but something he could hold in his hand. And he could swat them away just as easily.

He formed a giant hand, one of energy, translucent against the stars. His digits looked like tiny satellites or stars themselves, glowing and shining. His essence was comprised of the universe, and it created a mini-universe inside him.

Reaching out toward the battle, Drin grabbed one of the Sekaran vessels and crushed it in *his* hand. The ship exploded and crumpled. It was that simple. He *could* do anything with the Lord's help. Through the machine, Yezuah had given him unlimited power.

It was time to end this farce of a battle. The Elorians would be spared, God's people saved, in order that they might spread the good news of salvation to others. First, to the Arasu, and then to others. But he was getting ahead of himself. He had to finish this first.

In his cosmic hand, he formed a giant blade of light, so bright it would have been overwhelming on the surface of Arasu, washing out everything in its glowing radiance. This system's sun could not compare to Drin's sword.

He struck at the Sekaran capital ships. One by one, he disintegrated them with his blade, careful not to strike at their Elorian counterparts. Once the capital ships were gone, their fighters would be able to do little against the Elorian fleet. Drin cut through each of the larger vessels until there were none left. Space around Arasu turned into one giant debris field.

It would be enough. The battle was over. The rest would be clean up for his people. They would be overjoyed, and with their newfound confidence and faith in what Drin had done, they would truly be able to begin a new mission to change this galaxy. Faith would win.

He'd prevailed, but the energy expenditure proved far too much for him to maintain. He'd spent himself in the effort.

His form, however, couldn't handle all of the rapid change. Drin looked down at himself, only to see his limbs seeming to pixelate in real time. This couldn't be happening. He tensed, unable to do anything but watch. Was this the price he had to pay for power?

The stars shined through his hands, his entire form becoming translucent. With each breath, Drin faded into stardust.

His existence shimmered out into nothingness.

THIRTY-TWO

ANAIS AWOKE TO THE SOUND OF RUSTLING WIND BLOWING rocks and sand onto the Sekaran fighter. What had just happened? They were falling to their doom, with no possible way to slow the craft and get themselves to safety, and now they were on the ground?

Err-dio stirred behind her. He shuffled in his cockpit chair. "My Lord...what's going on? Where are we?"

"I'm not sure," Anais said. Her vision was cloudy from tears streaking down her face in the last moments before she'd lost consciousness. They appeared to be on Arasu, and they were parked in one of the canyons.

A group of Arasu approached them, armored, with weapons in their hands.

"We might have to get ready to fight," Anais said. The nanites had already formed her armor around her. She unstrapped herself from her chair. Would it be smart to open the hatch? It would expose Err-dio, but on the other hand, they were trapped in here.

"I've got my laser-repeater ready," Err-dio said.

The Arasu pointed their weapons at the craft, their leader

speaking through a megaphone. "Sekaran pilots, open your hatch and come out with your hands up. You are to be taken prisoner by the free Arasu. If you comply, you will not be harmed," he said.

"They think we're Sekarans," Err-dio said.

"Let's open the hatch and tell them we're not. These people are on our side!" Anais was relieved. She was so sick of battle, of killing. All she wanted to do was to go home.

The craft hatch popped open, pressure equalizing with the outside. Anais moved slowly, not wanting them to accidentally fire upon her because they became skittish. "Free Arasu, it's Anais, the Deklyn who assisted Cudree with his resistance."

The leader of the group stepped forward, holding a closed fist up to signify his men to hold their fire. "What are you doing in a Sekaran ship?"

"Let me come down, and I'll tell you everything."

The leader motioned to his men, who in turn set themselves at ease, no longer pointing their weapons toward the fighter. Anais stepped onto the rail of the cockpit and leaped down, letting her armor absorb the shock of the fall. Err-dio had to climb the ladder down the old-fashioned way but wasn't far behind her.

She shook the leader's hand, who introduced himself as Solee, and she told him about everything they did up on the Sekaran ship, and of their escape in the middle of the battle.

"You took great risks to defend my people," Solee said.

Anais almost told him she hadn't done it for her people, but she stopped herself. This was politics, right? And her world would want to make friends with these free Arasu, as sure as they had attempted to make trade negotiations before. Her thoughts drifted to Elaym, and she hoped he was doing well. It was fortunate he hadn't become entangled in the plot she had. Regardless, Anais might not have done her deeds completely for the Arasu people, but they were a part of it. "I'm glad to have helped," Anais said.

Solee lead them back into the city, where smoke rose from

various battles, some debris in the street from destroyed carts or windows which had taken fire. The damage didn't look all that severe, however. Not compared to the toll a war took on her home world of Deklyn.

They entered large building carved into the back of the rock face. Inside, Cudree and his men were setting up stations, monitoring the city and trying to do all they could to maintain order. Some dispatched soldiers to areas where the peace needed to be kept, others dispatched medics to help the wounded. Anais recalled in vivid detail the chaos of trying to manage a government directly after a battle. Cudree seemed to handle it well.

He handled some business with his people, and then Solee brought Anais and Err-dio before him. Cudree's antennae twitched at the sight of her. "You survived."

"You sound surprised," Anais said.

"After we gained control of the city, my people couldn't find any sign of you. We figured you had to have been disintegrated by the Sekarans," he said.

"It's a long story."

"No doubt," Cudree said. "We've managed to contain most of the traitors. If I had known so many of our people would be outraged by the prospect of their leaders working with Sekarans, I would have staged this revolution earlier. It went very well."

"I'm glad to hear it," Anais said. "What about the battle in space? Do we know how that went?"

Cudree walked to a wall display and changed the view to a spatial battle map. "It appears the Sekarans have been vanquished there, as well. It looked like they were going to be winning the day at first, but something strange happened. The Sekaran ships started exploding. I've never seen anything like it. There was no rhyme nor reason for it."

Drin, Anais thought. It had to have been his influence. Had he found some superweapon of his own and directed it at the Sekarans? She wished he was here with her.

"I'm readying our troops for Elorian invasion. I'm not sure we have the forces to be able to withstand them," Cudree said in a dejected tone.

"Don't worry about them," Anais said. "They'll come peacefully. I'm sure they'll want to speak to you and your people about their religion, but they won't force it upon you. Not like the Sekarans."

"Are you sure?" Cudree asked.

Err-dio nodded. "I can vouch for them personally. They liberated our world and left the choice to us. There is a compelling reason to listen to them. I would urge you to do so."

"We'll deal with that when the time comes, then," Cudree said. "It's a relief to hear I won't have to be directing my people into yet another battle."

Anais surveyed the room. All the Arasu worked hard. It was a relief that this battle was over, however Drin had managed to do it. "I'm hoping our worlds can be friends. Your first representative, Zebee, had worked out a deal with our world where we would be able to trade with one another. I hope, even though his motives weren't pure, the offer will still stand?"

Cudree's bug face was as expressionless as it always appeared. Anais still couldn't make out anything about these people. "Of course. We would be happy to extend our friendship to you and your world, especially with all the help you've given us here."

"Thank you," Anais said. She glanced to Err-dio, who stood with all six arms at his side, waiting patiently as ever. He was about the best guardian she could have asked for, loyal to a tee and never asking anything of her. "We had a companion. He went into the caves the last we saw him, and we want to try to go find him."

"Do you need any men to accompany you?" Cudree asked.

"I don't think so. The Sekarans are gone, yes?" Anais shrugged.

"When we return, though, I'd appreciate a shuttle to take us to my world. As hospitable as you are, I need to get home."

"Whatever resources we can provide are yours," Cudree said. He went back to his tasks with many others in the room waiting to get in a word with him. He'd secured leadership, and he would be busy for a long time to come.

Anais and Err-dio departed, saying their goodbyes to Solee, who took his men out on patrol to look for any more straggling Sekarans. Anais and Err-dio walked through the city streets alone. She recalled the way to the crack in the cave, which led to a deeper cavern system. "I hope Drin's okay," Anais said.

"He is," Err-dio said. "Have faith."

They didn't need to walk for long. Pink energy descended upon the street, covering everything in its radiant glow. It breathed in and out, much like a heartbeat. The energy swirled into a whirl-wind, forcing Anais to cover her face.

When the wind stopped, she looked again, and saw Drin standing before her. His green face held a stoic expression, but there was a weariness in his eyes she had never seen from him. He looked as if he were struggling to stand.

Even if he were injured or tired, what mattered was, he lived. She squeaked, an awkward sound in her excitement, but she didn't care. He was here. He lived! Anais ran forward and threw her arms around him.

Drin hugged her in return, his strong arms around her waist. Thank God he was here. She didn't know what she'd do without him. To her surprise, he leaned his head in and kissed her.

The shock of his gesture nearly made her faint. He'd been so adamant against any sort of physical connection between them, and now?

The kiss couldn't be said to be one of expertise. His lips moved awkwardly, and they parted with little confidence. He recoiled, breaking the kiss. It was too foreign to him, she could feel it through the nanites, and she could see it in his deep eyes.

Despite its inexperience, the kiss held a fiery passion to it that made the kiss a moment that shook Anais from the tips of her ears down to her toes. His tender care melted her. She wanted to go limp in his arms and have him hold her forever. It was beautiful. He was beautiful. Did he know?

Drin merely smiled at her, eyes focused on her, adoring, loving, stable. Everything she ever wanted.

Anais tilted her head upward at him, her reverie broken by confusion. "What about—"

Before she could finish the question, Drin answered, "Yezuah has made it clear to me there is no shame in my love for you. Man was designed to love woman. I have taken vows to the Church in the past, but they have been superseded by a new covenant with me. I am Templar no more. I am the Lord's harbinger."

She couldn't say she well understood what he was saying, but she nodded nonetheless. Then, she remembered Err-dio was there. He stood to the side, pacing back and forth and glancing at the buildings as if surveying the architecture. The sight made Anais chuckle. "I don't understand," she said to Drin.

"I don't entirely, either. It will come in time, or it won't. Whatever the Lord wills. Through my faith, I've gained power like I had never been able to imagine. These next days will be interesting times," Drin said.

Err-dio stepped toward them. "Was that how you destroyed the Sekaran fleet? It was you. I knew it."

Drin nodded, breaking his embrace with Anais. "I did what I had to do. There's much to reflect on. I wish to take the time to rest and meditate. Though I have power, it's taking everything in me to be able to stand here." he glanced upward, as if seeing something through the rock face that covered the city. "But I'm afraid before I can recover, I'll have to meet with my people."

"You'll be leaving me again," Anais said.

Drin frowned. "Perhaps. Perhaps not. I'm not certain how events will transpire. There is one possibility. You could merge yourself with what I've become. I can't explain it because I don't understand it myself. Soon."

The prospect was too much for Anais. She wasn't sure what he'd become, but he was talking strangely. He was still Drin, but different. "I don't know if I'd be ready for it."

"Understandable," Drin said. "If you choose to, the offer will always be open. I am yours for eternity, Anais."

If his kiss and his touch hadn't already melted her, Anais would have been in Heaven. She could hardly believe what she was hearing. It was so much change, so fast. She found herself fanning her face as her cheeks had become so hot. "And I'm yours," she managed to get out.

Drin's visage faded before her. Was it only some pale reflection of him, like a holo? She couldn't be certain. He looked at peace as his body disappeared, and more of the pink energy formed.

"Goodbye, Drin," Anais said.

"Not goodbye. Merely so long for now." He disappeared.

EPILOGUE

A BURST OF ENERGY FORMED IN FRONT OF THE ELORIAN SHIP, *Compassion,* which had landed on a high mesa on Arasu. A ramp descended, allowing several Templars to exit, along with Elorian infantry regulars. With them was a man in long, cloth robes, the Father and leader of the ship. As the energy intensified, it blinded the Elorians. They covered their faces and recoiled. Some closed their eyes and dropped to their knees, praying and begging forgiveness.

The energy coalesced into one of them, an Elorian form. A former Templar turned harbinger of God.

"Save your prayers for the one true God," Drin said.

The soldiers slowly opened their eyes and turned their gazes to him. Confusion crossed the faces of many. The father stepped forward, boldly stepping in front of Drin. "What is this witch-craft?" he asked.

Drin held his ground, expressionless. "No witchcraft. The power of the one true God. The nanites flow through me as they do many of your Templars. They can verify this."

One of the Templars stepped forward, wearing his traditional

Elorian battle armor. He reached out with his nanite energy field, the little machines mingling with the edge of Drin's. Unlike when he and Anais had shared a moment, Drin kept himself closed off. He would be able to sense much more from this Elorian than he would reveal.

The Templar was afraid, as he had every right to be. They'd been in one of the biggest battles of all time, and it had ended because of an act of God. Now, he stood before someone who could appear from thin air. Drin had some sympathy for the man.

"He has the nanites," the Templar said.

The father cocked his head curiously to peer at Drin. "Who are you?"

"I am Drin, formerly of the *Justicar,*" Drin said.

The father's eyes softened. "I am sorry for the loss of your brothers and sisters aboard. I'm Father Nohl."

The other Elorians shuffled about as another man descended from the ramp of the *Compassion.* His robes were much more ornate than the father's, crimson with white trim and tassels. He was an older man, somewhat portlier than everyone else, with a round face and droopy eyes. Cardinal Levy, the church official Drin had petitioned for reinforcements.

"Templar Drin," Cardinal Levy said.

Despite Drin being so much more than a Templar, he took a knee before the cardinal. He had a duty to the church, even still. It was his job to serve and to be an example for the others. To wield power and not become corrupt, one had to humble himself.

"Arise, my son," Cardinal Levy said.

Drin stood once more. With the cardinal present, none of the Elorians dared move. All were focused on him. It wasn't every day someone could meet a cardinal. Had this been a month ago, Drin might have been shaking in his boots, but after he'd interacted with Yezuah, meeting someone of the cardinal's stature proved to be easy.

"You summoned us here because you knew the Sekarans would be attacking. It took much deliberation as to whether we should come or not, but after prayer, the cardinals and the Pope came to a unanimous decision to bring our greatest warships here. Such a large force together has only occurred a few times in history," he said.

"I know," Drin said.

"Are you aware of how the battle transpired? The miracle of the Lord's hand vanquishing His enemies?" the cardinal asked.

"I am. The miracle was brought forth by my own hand," Drin said.

Someone gasped. Cardinal Levy held a hand backward as if to tell the soldier to hold his tongue. "You make quite the claim, Drin, though from your performance arriving here, I see no cause to doubt you."

"My hand is guided by the Lord. I serve only Him." It should be obvious, but he figured it would be best to clarify.

Before the cardinal could say more, a rumbling came from above, the sound of thrusters. Wind picked up as a ship descended from the sky. This one was one of the sleekest Drin had ever seen, with reflective metal, which gave a camouflaged sense to it. The ship was thin geometrically, long, coming to a point at the nose, and with two side compartments. It was much smaller than the Elorian warship it landed beside. The ship was the most recognizable among all the Elorian fleet, however—The Pope's Holy Vessel.

Guards exited from the ship, clad completely in white cloth, each with dual light sword hilts hanging from their hips. Their clothing was immaculate and ornate, even in its pure white color form, which only served to accent their dark green skin. They wore no armor, for they understood God protected them at all times in their duty. Four of the guards marched forward, two by two, until stopping and parting, making way for the Pope to come between them.

A very old Elorian, hunched, almost frail looking, stepped from the craft. He stood on a small, circular hoverpad, which brought him forward through the nanites' power. He moved between his guards and landed the hoverpad.

Everyone knelt. Pope Fayr XXII lifted his frail arms, wrinkled and shaking from the strain. "Lord God Yezuah, bless your holy children in this day. Keep us pure in all we do as we continue this spiritual battle to bring peace to this universe. The power and glory yours forever."

"Amen," muttered the Elorians present.

"You may rise," Pope Fayr said. His eyes set on Drin. They were aged ones, deep, much like the Lord Yezuah's in understanding. He took steps forward down the ramp, very carefully, nearly falling from the strain. One of the guards moved to help him, but the Pope waved the guard off. He slowly approached Drin.

Drin understood the reason the Pope had come here. It was for him. He stood straight as he could, as if ready for inspection from his superiors. The thought made him recall how Commander Shayne would pick apart even the littlest detail in order to snap his Templars into discipline. He longed for those simpler days.

Pope Fayr came very close to him, his breath on Drin's face, looking Drin directly in the eye. He reached up and placed a hand on Drin's forehead. The wrinkled hands were calloused, abrasive to the touch. Drin held still.

"You have had great power bestowed upon you," Pope Fayr said.

"I have," Drin said.

"It was foretold in the ultimate prophecy, 'a harbinger will come to my people, one to lead them beyond the stars. His mighty hand will sweep aside planets and stars, and his gaze will cause my enemies to tremble.'"

"Blessed is the holy prophecy," Drin said out of habit.

"Are you the one come to fulfill this prophecy?"

The question was a difficult one. Drin had no idea. He only did what he felt compelled to do by the Lord. He also wasn't sure how to answer. To say yes felt like hubris, something he didn't want to display.

You are my chosen vessel, the voice said within him.

Then it would be so. "Yes," Drin said.

"Bold words. They have been stated by many a man over the centuries. Every time the end times were said to be coming, they have proved to be false. We are not supposed to guess or presume to know the time and place of God's return," Pope Fayr said.

"If we are not to know when it is happening, and yet it supposed to fulfill the scriptures, how can it happen?"

Pope Fayr laughed. "The great mystery of life and faith." He drew his hand back. "I believe you have a gift from God within you. I have witnessed with my own eyes the results of the battle above. The Lord is at work here. We have removed a great threat from the galaxy, and this leaves us with the question—what comes next?"

"I wouldn't presume to—"

Pope Fayr shook his head. "No, you wouldn't. But I am asking you, as an instrument of the Lord, because I have faith."

Drin paused, then nodded. The truth was clear. God had instilled the knowledge in him. It was not time to fret or worry, but time to be bold. "I believe the end times are upon us," he said.

More gasps came from soldiers. Some considered it blasphemy, but it didn't matter. Drin had to speak the truth as he saw it.

"The Sekarans have destroyed a whole world. The battle is certainly escalating," Pope Fayr said.

"We have vanquished their superweapon," Drin said. "Now, for the first time in centuries, it's time for the Elorians to go on the offensive rather than biding our time and reacting to Sekaran moves. This is the crusade we're being called to," Drin said. The words resonated as he said them. It was like his lips were moving, but they were not his own. God was in control now. "It's time to assert ourselves as the one Holy Church, and let the galaxy know the way to salvation."

"And how do you propose we do this?" Pope Fayr asked.

Drin cast his eyes to all present. So many afraid. Even more confused. They would calm in time. They had to. He would instill confidence in them like they hadn't had in generations, when the gospel was first being spread to other worlds. The church would be great once more. "It's time to retake Eloria."

The words shocked everyone into silence, but then several of the soldiers clapped. It was followed by more rousing cheers. "Retake Eloria!" others called. "God wills it!" The sentiment brought a chilling joy around which Drin could sense. But his people were with him. They had faith, as they'd seen the results of this battle. And with faith, what couldn't they accomplish?

Pope Fayr turned to address them all. "You heard your brother. I have had visions that confirm what he is saying. The Lord is telling us he is on the move, and we will move with him." He lifted his hands toward the sky once more. "Lord, bless us in this day, keep your harbinger close so he may guide us in wisdom and bring about the joy of your eternal kingdom." He lowered his hands and turned back toward Drin.

"On to The Final Battle," Drin said.

Those words held weight. The Pope nodded and gazed at Drin expectantly.

It was up to him.

You can do even more through me.

He could. He had no doubts about it now. Drin closed his eyes and focused. His body shattered into its energy form once more, and he spread himself throughout the entire area. He could sense the thoughts of all the soldiers and Templars with him. They were scared. He willed them not to be afraid, hoping the message came through to them. Light radiated from him, engulfing everything around him. He gathered up the men, the ships, the weapons, the Elorian vessels surrounding the planet, and he pushed his reach even further.

Elorian bases, the other fleets, they would all be needed. They had to gather together, to become one, to fight as one Holy Church. In unity, they would be their strongest. Drin grew himself, stretching and spreading his energy and essence out into the stars, cradling his people as if they were but babes in his arms. Some resisted at first, none were ready. But it didn't matter. They had faith. This was the day they were all waiting for since Yezuah had first shed his blood on the Mount of Alms.

The Spirit of Yezuah filled him then, guiding his actions, his thoughts. He let the Lord take control. *Not my will, but Yours be done,* Drin thought.

They would go onward to fight The Final Battle, the army of God. Nothing could stop them.

Continue Jon Del Arroz's epic space opera adventures with his hit series, The Aryshan War and the first book The Stars Entwined.

The Stars Entwined

Alarms blared. Warning lights flashed from the side of the cockpit. Regus Jackson shook his head to purge the grogginess from his eyes. He sat up straight, gripping the arms of his chair.

"What the hell is going on?" How long had he been asleep? He glanced to the sidewall chrono—over two hours.

"We have an incoming ship gaining on us." Ellund tapped controls. An overlay window opened on the screen. A plot-point map projected the other ship's trajectory in relation to the *Sunflower*. "They'll overtake us in five minutes."

"What kind of ship?" Regus asked. His palm slipped on the metal armrest. He wiped his sweat on his pant leg. It wasn't hot in here. Nerves were getting the best of him.

"What do you think?" Ellund asked, irritation seeping into his voice. This crew never handled tense situations well. They'd had shouting matches in the past, usually over foolish matters. It would do no good to shout now.

"Aryshans," Regus muttered under his breath. He had made the decision to take the shorter trade route through this sector to make up for lost time spent at their last port. It had been a calculated risk, but there shouldn't have been any other ships this far into open space. "Bill, can we shake them?"

Bill shook his head. "I don't know anything about Aryshans, but we got a piece of junk here that's barely spaceworthy. We do have an incoming communication, text only."

"Display it."

Another window layered on the screen, this time with text: *Human vessel. Turn around. Return to your space.*

A simple enough demand, but they were now two hours of fuel into the journey and a return trajectory would set them even further back if they had to go around. He had to think quickly. "Tell them... Hmm," Bill said, stroking his chin. He snapped his fingers. "I got it. Tell them our crystal drive is stuck engaged. It's going to take some time for us to fix."

Bill typed into his keyboard and sent the message.

The three men stared at the screen, waiting. Hopefully, the Aryshans bought the story.

"Another message," Bill said.

The display on the screen changed. *Reverse course. No further delays.*

"I think we should do as they say, boss," Ellund said.

The *Sunflower* jolted forward as if it had collided with something. Regus dug his feet into the metal plating on the floor to stay in his chair. On his armrest display, the crystal drive schematic blinked red. They had a real problem.

"Now what?" Regus asked.

"Drive failure. We're going to need a reboot and... Oh, damn."

The screen switched to a view of a massive Aryshan ship only just avoiding collision with the *Sunflower*. It would look to them as if the *Sunflower* had intentionally tried to hit them. This couldn't be good.

"Send apologies, quickly!" Regus said.

"I'm working on it," Bill said, typing frantically. Alarms blared again.

"They fired on us!" Ellund shouted. He jumped from his seat, ready to flee, but there was nowhere to go. Like a trapped animal, he stared at Regus.

Crossing into Aryshan space had been a terrible decision. He should never have pressed his luck like this. The incoming projectiles loomed on the map, taunting him, seeming to take an eternity to reach the *Sunflower*. It was the last thing Regus Jackson would ever see.

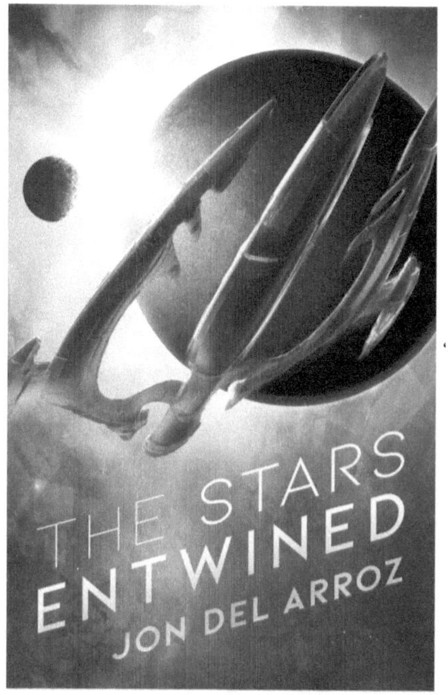

Earth needs a spy...

...is he prepared?

Lieutenant Sean Barrows is thrust into a plot of sabotage and destruction brought on by the mysterious Aryshan Empire.

His assignment: to infiltrate an enemy warship to bring his superiors information on their destructive capabilities and battle plans.

But the Ayrshans share telepathic bonds which make them paranoid of outsiders, and try as he may to win the heart of a beautiful Aryshan commander, he can only get so close.

To make matters worse, Earth stands on the brink of destruction as the Aryshans develop a new, invisible weapon.

Fans of The Old Man's War by John Scalzi and The Ember War by

Richard Fox will love this epic space opera. Read The Stars Entwined
today!

REVIEW REQUEST

Did you enjoy the book?

Why not tell others about it? The best way to help an author and to spread word about books you love is to leave a review.

If you enjoyed reading GLORIFIED, can you please leave a review on Amazon for it? Good, bad, or mediocre, we want to hear from *you*. Jon and all of us at Rislandia Books would greatly appreciate it.

Thank you!

ABOUT JON DEL ARROZ

Jon Del Arroz is a #1 Amazon Bestselling author, "the leading Hispanic voice in science fiction" according to PJMedia.com, and winner of the 2018 CLFA Book Of The Year Award. As a contributor to The Federalist, he is also recognized as a popular journalist and cultural commentator. Del Arroz writes science fiction, steampunk, and comic books, and can be found most weekends in section 127 of the Oakland Coliseum cheering on the A's.

Keep up with Jon on his YouTube channel.

GLORIFIED

SAGA OF THE NANO TEMPLAR, BOOK THREE

By Jon Del Arroz

Rislandia Books

✵ Created with Vellum